How did she thank him for saving her from certain death?

The tenderness and concern she saw on his face was too much. Rick had never looked at her that way before.

His gaze locked on hers, searching, questioning.

She couldn't let herself be in his arms anymore, and she worked to free herself from his protective embrace. "Let me go, Rick. They're gone now."

His eyes widened, as though he hadn't realized he'd been holding her. He crawled over and slowly peeked through the brush that blocked his vision.

Was she wrong? Had someone stayed behind to see if they'd survived the crash, after all? Her pulse pounded in her neck. *Breathe...just breathe.*

"Rick, you're scaring me. Why are you still looking for them? They're gone, right? Please tell me they're gone."

He stilled. "For now."

Books by Elizabeth Goddard

Love Inspired Suspense

Freezing Point
Treacherous Skies
Riptide
Wilderness Peril

ELIZABETH GODDARD

is a seventh-generation Texan who grew up in a small oil town in East Texas, surrounded by Christian family and friends. Becoming a writer of Christian fiction was a natural outcome of her love of reading, fueled by a strong faith.

Elizabeth attended the University of North Texas, where she received her degree in computer science. She spent the next seven years working in high-level sales for a software company located in Dallas, traveling throughout the United States and Canada as part of the job. At twenty-five, she finally met the man of her dreams and married him a few short weeks later. When she had her first child, she moved back to East Texas with her husband and daughter and worked for a pharmaceutical company. But then more children came along, and it was time to focus on family. Elizabeth loves that she gets to do her favorite things every day—read, write novels, stay at home with her four precious children and work with her adoring husband in ministry.

WILDERNESS PERIL

ELIZABETH GODDARD

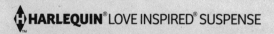

HARLEQUIN® LOVE INSPIRED® SUSPENSE

™ LOVE INSPIRED BOOKS

PLEASE RECYCLE
THIS PRODUCT IS RECYCLABLE

Recycling programs
for this product may
not exist in your area.

ISBN-13: 978-0-373-67588-3

WILDERNESS PERIL

Copyright © 2013 by Elizabeth Goddard

This edition published by arrangement with Love Inspired Books.

® and TM are trademarks of Love Inspired Books, used under license.
Trademarks indicated with ® are registered in the United States Patent
and Trademark Office, the Canadian Trade Marks Office and in other
countries.

www.Harlequin.com

Printed in U.S.A.

They triumphed over him by the blood of the Lamb
and by the word of their testimony; they did not love
their lives so much as to shrink from death.
—*Revelation* 12:11

This book is dedicated to my Lord and Savior Jesus Christ, who died that we might live. Who said, "Greater love has no one than this, that he lay down his life for his friends" (John 15:13). And to those who have gone before and serve even now in the armed forces, laying down their lives so we might live, and live freely.

ONE

Interior Alaska

"Did your brother ever show?" Shay Ridiker asked as she climbed into the passenger seat of an old rusty Jeep Cherokee. She fought to keep her voice calm and to shake off the eerie, uncomfortable feeling that she was being watched.

She might be one of the best aircraft mechanics around and people might think she was tough because of it, but that didn't mean she could handle a day of travel to Nowhere, Alaska, without her nerves starting to kick in, especially if there was a chance they would have to face trouble.

And trouble was exactly what she saw in Rick Savage's gunmetal grays. "No," he said.

Aiden Savage—a fellow employee of Deep Horizon Recovery Services—was supposed to have met them two hours ago to lead them to the plane he had come to Alaska to repossess—only it needed a mechanic, hence why Aiden had asked for Shay's help. They'd arrived to find no sign of him. But Aiden… He had a few troubles. Wasn't always the most dependable person, and maybe this was one of those times.

Rick's brother had struggled with alcohol abuse in the past, but Connor Jacobson, the owner of Deep Horizon Recovery Services, had given him a break because he'd served in the armed forces like Connor—the guy had a big heart and was all about second chances. Aiden had been sober for a year now and definitely deserved that chance. And as far as she knew, in the time that he'd worked for Deep Horizon, he'd never let Connor down.

Something was wrong.

"Maybe someone's onto us taking the plane." And had prevented Aiden from meeting them.

"Maybe."

Shay rubbed her forehead. His one-word answers were getting to her. Obviously, he was thinking things through and didn't want her opinion. Either that or he didn't want to tell her everything.

Behind the wheel, Rick shifted into Drive and urged the vehicle he'd begged or borrowed for the day out of the dark alley where he'd parked and onto the street. The beautiful, sunny autumn day seemed to contradict the uneasiness spilling off Rick.

Their short visit to Alaska wouldn't allow Shay to experience the midnight sun or inordinately long nights since it was September, and for that she was thankful. But it was the only thing she could find to be thankful about this trip. Shay wasn't a wilderness girl. She might be a mechanic, but she didn't like roughing it.

Rick steered away from the general store and the hostel next door that provided meager accommodations for the few who traveled into Alaska's interior. A glance into the backseat revealed their bags and coats. Rick hadn't checked them into the hostel as planned?

"Your tools, the replacement part for the plane, they're in the back," he said.

Shay blew out a breath. "So that's why you got the wheels? We're going to look for him? As in drive some wilderness back roads?"

"Yes." Rick focused on the road, his voice gruff, concerned.

When Rick's brother had called from Alaska to say that the plane they were supposed to repossess had a mechanical problem, it had been easy for Shay to diagnose the problem as an exhaust leak. The hard part had come when it was decided that she'd have to go out in person to fix it. Add that the plane was in the middle of the Alaskan bush and it was decided that Rick would escort her to meet his brother.

"He'll make sure you get there safely," Shay's boss, Connor, had said.

Somehow, remembering those words didn't make her feel any better now. Rick's semiautomatic rested on the seat between them, but even that didn't give her a sense of security. She had her reasons for disliking guns. Besides, Shay and that particular weapon had a past together that she wanted to forget.

Shay was beginning to think she'd made a big mistake in agreeing to this. She'd only given in after Connor's assurances that she'd be in no danger. Though the Deep Horizon crew occasionally retrieved property in high-risk situations, that didn't happen too often. Nor had Aiden mentioned any concerns or potential problems.

This was a small plane he'd gone to get. Usually, they only saw trouble when they had to retrieve Learjets and jumbo jets from rich people and bad guys in third-world countries. Buster Kemp wasn't either of those, at least on paper. So what had happened to make Aiden disappear? And why did she feel so uneasy?

The Jeep crept along the gravel road of the simple village, barely a town and mostly populated by native Alaskans from a tribe Shay couldn't pronounce. Rick kept going once they'd passed the last of the buildings that made up the town—the only representation of civilization for a good hundred-mile radius.

Shay didn't like the idea of heading for the Alaskan wilderness until she knew more.

A lot more.

But it wasn't as if she and Rick could just go home and come back later. Getting there had already been a two-day journey, starting with a flight from Nebraska to Seattle, then another flight to Fairbanks and finally a ride out on a seaplane mail flight to this remote village.

Until now, Shay's job description hadn't included being put in the field. She liked working behind the scenes. Yet here she was.

"Why are we going to trek through the wilderness to look for him when we don't even know where the plane is? That's why he wanted us to wait for him—so he could show us where to go."

"Well, he's not here. Just what do you want me to do?"

"I don't know. Ask around?" When Aiden had been late in meeting them, Shay had left Rick to wait for his brother while she hung out at the general store, looking at all the handcrafted beadwork and turquoise jewelry created by the local natives for the tourists.

"What do you think I've been doing? I asked around. Nobody knows anything. Nobody has seen him, of course. We make it our job to slip in and out, remember? To be invisible."

She frowned, hating that she'd not given Rick the benefit of the doubt. Of course he would have already covered the basics.

Peering through the back window, Shay watched the town of Tanaken growing distant. She resisted the urge to say that they should get back on that seaplane when it returned and head back to Fairbanks. She knew that wasn't going to happen. Not without Rick's brother, Aiden.

Not without that plane that he'd come to retrieve that Shay could only hope hadn't been lost through a flare-up of Aiden's old problem.

"I can honestly say I was hoping to find him drunk somewhere." Rick rubbed his temple, worked his jaw. "That'd be better than the other scenarios running through my mind."

Shay wanted to reach over and squeeze his shoulder. Her heart went out to the guy, and for more than his missing brother. But he scared her, too. He kept too much bottled up inside him, and she'd seen it explode at the wrong time.

"He's had troubles in the past, but there are good reasons for that." He sighed like an Alaskan facing more snow after a record-setting storm. "He wouldn't just disappear like this, not with us coming to meet him."

"So talk to the sheriff, then."

His half laugh sounded forced. "They don't have sheriffs in Alaska. Out in the bush, they have village public safety officers. When I asked around, I was told she was helping deliver a baby, so I left it at that."

"Are you kidding me?"

"I wish I were. Besides, Aiden hasn't been gone long enough to cause concern for the authorities. But I'm still worried. Something about this job hasn't felt right to me from the start."

Shay gazed over her shoulder and stared out the back window again.

"That's why I brought the gun. I had a feeling." He tossed a glance her way. "You ever have one of those?"

Shay angled her head to look at Rick while she considered his question. When the light hit his eyes just right, the gray almost looked blue. With his thick brown sun-kissed hair, the tanned skin of a man who spent a lot of time in the sun, his toned physique and the way he handled himself— Oh, yeah, she had a few feelings herself.

But attraction wasn't where the feelings ended, and that was the problem. She'd also had a feeling that Rick Savage would never notice her, and so far he hadn't disappointed. That was okay, because seeing the pain her father went through after losing her mother, Shay didn't want to fall in love. Shay was all about staying safe, and love wasn't a safe choice. Especially not with a man like Rick. That had been especially true after the day he pointed a gun at her.

"I've had a few feelings, sure, like the one I have right now that I'm not going to like where we're going. It's not like we can get too far on wheels in the direction you're heading." Oh, yeah, she'd looked at the maps of Alaska, all right.

"There has to be an airstrip somewhere around here or else there couldn't be an airplane. I didn't mention anything to the seaplane's bush pilot because I didn't want him to know what we were up to, but I did ask an old-timer, a native Alaskan woman, who looked like she'd been around long enough to know something."

"And?" Shay's question was accompanied by a jolt.

The shocks on this Jeep were in serious need of repair. She'd never liked Jeeps as it was. Squeezing the handgrip, she pressed her other palm against the top of the cab, but her head bumped the ceiling anyway.

Rick tugged a piece of paper from his pocket and handed it over. She recognized his handwriting and read the lengthy, convoluted directions.

"Directions to a gold-mining claim? Are you serious?"

"Dead serious."

Shay sat up, not liking where any of this was taking them. "What aren't you telling me?"

Rick exhaled. "Someone's been watching us. Following me around. They were getting a little too close for comfort."

Shay didn't speak for a few seconds. Rick cut her a glance, catching her frown. Did she think he was overreacting? He couldn't tell. He'd never spent this much time with her, especially in such close quarters, so he had no experience reading her expressions. Looking for clues into her thoughts, his eyes skimmed over the few freckles splashed across her nose and the short-cropped auburn hair framing her face that was a little mussed from their travels.

"You think it's related to Aiden and the plane? Why don't you just ask them instead of running away?"

Rick shot her a glance. "I did."

Shay's sunset-blue eyes grew wide with her gasp. "And what did they say?"

"Let's just say they weren't forthcoming with answers. They made a wrong move and I had to make a fast exit. That's when I came for you."

He glanced her way and she watched him. He didn't like the look of concern on her face. "Not to worry. We lost them."

For now, at least—but depending on what they

wanted, he could expect to see them again. Were they bent on stopping them from taking the plane? Did they know something about Aiden? Or were they just a couple of guys preying on tourists in backcountry Alaska? If something happened to him, then what about Shay? What would she do? He'd tried to find out what he could in town but when they'd grabbed him, thinking he was an easy target, he'd opted to leave them behind and come for Shay.

The trick would be to stay safe until they could find Aiden or make it out of here on the next bush flight tomorrow—whichever came first.

The Jeep bounced to the right, and Rick turned his focus to the uneven dirt road—a thirty-five-mile loop to a secluded lake. He wasn't sure he wanted to endure the bumpy road for another thirty-plus miles, and he doubted Shay would be too happy with the journey either, but there was strength behind her beauty. He knew she could handle it.

She sighed and stared at the paper with directions. He knew she was probably still worried about those men. He could only be grateful she wasn't with him when the confrontation had happened. They could have easily used her against him in that situation, and then where would they be?

"This looks like it's going to be the scenic route," she finally said. "What happens when we get to the nine-mile ridge trail? Don't we need ATVs or something? How're we going to get there?"

"I suspect there's an easier way in, but those directions are all I have for now." If anyone was actually mining the claim, as his conversation with the woman had made him suspect, they'd have had to have built a road to move in the type of equipment used these days. But if something sinister was going on and his brother was in trouble, going in the direct way would be a mistake. The roundabout path would be their best bet.

"Rick," Shay said, startling him out of his thoughts.

He realized now that she'd been talking to him for a while and he hadn't been listening. Looking over at her, he sent her a look like he'd heard every word. "Just focusing on the road, thinking about the directions."

Hoping I wrote them down right.

"These directions aren't a stroll in the park," Shay said. "Unless you've done a lot of shopping, we're not prepared to get to this claim. Haven't you heard a word I've said?" Her gaze skewered him, burning a hole through his head.

"I just want to drive the loop to get a look and feel, okay?"

If he was brave enough to stare her down at the moment, he might risk a look into her eyes. Back at the Deep Horizon shop, any time Shay explained some sort of complicated repair she was making, Rick would get lost in those eyes, then shake himself free and pretend he'd been listening. Just like he'd been doing now. He had a feeling he hadn't fooled her then.

Or fooled her now.

She slapped his arm.

"Hey, what was that for?" He grimaced, making sure she witnessed it.

"What are the plans? I don't like being left out."

"Let's check it out—or as close to it as we can get in the Jeep. See if we can find Aiden. Maybe he's at the airstrip waiting for us and we just got our signals crossed." Now, *that* was like Aiden.

Something in the rearview mirror caught Rick's attention. *Uh-oh.* "We've got company."

Shay twisted in the seat to see. "We can't be the only ones traveling this road. They're probably just heading home for the day."

"Or maybe it's the same two men who gave me trouble. Let's test your theory and see if they come after us." He punched the accelerator.

The engine roared to life and echoed the truck behind them as it raced forward, gaining on them. That was a bad sign. A very bad sign.

His weapon bounced on the seat and almost out of reach, but Shay caught it.

"You know how to use one of those?"

"My daddy taught me how to shoot. How to fire a weapon at a target after…"

The way she trailed off, as though her mind was a million miles away, made Rick wonder what had happened. He wanted to her to finish the sentence.

"But aiming at a living, breathing human is different," she said, redirecting her thought.

She'd left something out.

Apprehension reflected in her expression. She understood what he'd truly been asking when he'd wanted to know if she could shoot. If they had to face off with the men in the truck behind them, and things got bad, could she pull that trigger?

As a marine helicopter pilot, he'd already had the experience of firing his weapon at living, breathing souls and knew he could do it. But he'd hoped to leave those days behind. Still, he wasn't going to dump the responsibility onto the woman by his side who wasn't trained for the job.

"Hand it over," he said, and pressed the gun against his thigh in the seat.

Behind him, the truck's lionesque roar grew louder as it gained on them.

TWO

"I suppose it's too late to turn around." Shay held tight to the edge of her seat to keep from getting bounced around, but her effort felt as futile as her words.

His focus on driving, Rick didn't respond, but her question was mostly rhetorical. His frown seemed to engulf his strong features as he worked his jaw, the muscles in his neck straining. If anyone could get them out of this, Rick could, but this situation looked more than out of their league, if you asked her.

Still, what did she know? Maybe it was only out of *her* league. Rick had served his country in the Middle East. Probably in worse situations than this.

The road grew shoddier the farther they went, the thick evergreens closing in around them, and the incline began to rise, making Shay more uncomfortable. Her knuckles turned white, she gripped the seat so hard.

Rick whipped the vehicle around a corner too fast and the force pressed Shay against her door. She was more than glad it was locked, safe and secure.

"This thing had better not roll."

The Jeep bucked and bounced next to a ridge—the drop a hundred feet at least. Her face pressed to the window, Shay yelled at him to be careful. But she didn't scream. She'd never hear the end of it back at the shop if she dared to act "girlie." Never. If they even made it back to the shop.

"Okay." She gasped for air. "Did you get a good look at them? Was it the same ones who followed you in the village?"

"I think so, yes."

"What would happen if we just stopped and faced off with them? Find out what they want. This is crazy."

"That's a bad idea," he said. "We've lost them for a minute. Time for a new game plan."

Suddenly, Rick shifted into four-wheel drive and started up an incline to their left, squeezing between trees. She could only suppose that the plan was for their pursuers to make the corner and miss them completely, clueless to the fact that Rick and Shay had turned off the road and made their own path up the side of the mountain.

Shay glanced behind them, and just beyond the ridge they'd almost tumbled from, she could see for miles. A river splashed over boulders and there was a lake a few miles out. Was that where they'd been headed? Or was that the lake near Tanaken?

But she couldn't see an airstrip. The trees were too thick; they hid it from her at this angle. While the Jeep traversed the mountain, the grade growing steeper by the second, Shay imagined the vehicle just falling, much like the feeling she'd had on the steep streets of San Francisco.

I'm going to be sick. Rick's going to know the truth—that I'm not so tough at all.

Connor would find out, and that would be the end of her job. He hadn't been easy to convince she could do such a physically demanding job in a man-dominated field. But what did that matter if they didn't get out of this? She squeezed her eyes shut, breathing too hard and fast. Her stomach rolled as if she were on an amusement-park ride.

Releasing her grip, Shay shifted forward and held her face to her hands against her lap and groaned. When would this be over?

Suddenly, it all stopped. Shay's silent cries had been answered.

Rick's warm hand gently squeezed her shoulder. "Hey. You okay?"

She sucked in a few more breaths, slower now, until finally, she could breathe normally. She hated he'd had to see that, and she sat up to peer at him. "No, I'm not all right. Are you?" She glared at him. He'd better not tell her he was fine.

The concern swimming in his eyes surprised her. He frowned. "I only meant… You seemed… Never mind."

Turning the other way, he studied their surroundings. Shay joined him. Her heart was still in her throat, but at least she could breathe now. Breathe…and think of the consequences of her little breakdown.

He'd seen right through her. She'd always been tough, self-sufficient. Never shown any weakness. She hated that Rick saw her vulnerable now. In the military, Rick was accustomed to being surrounded by strong women, so he expected nothing less from Shay. This was the first time he'd seen the weakness she'd worked so hard to hide. Resentment over that, compounded with the fear she'd felt when the men had chased them, made her want to snarl at Rick.

"Why are they after us, Rick? What in the

world is going on? You don't think they're trying to keep us from getting that plane, do you?"

"It seems like too much trouble for that. Why chase us down like this when all they have to do is keep us from taking it? That's why we should try to sneak in—so we won't have to have a confrontation, with or without guns."

"So what's the plan, then?"

"We wait until I'm sure we've lost them." Rick examined his weapon and chambered a round. "Then I'll get you back to the village as soon as I can. You're getting on the next plane out of here. Unfortunately, that probably won't be until morning."

"But…there's a plane that I'm supposed to repair, and then we can all three fly out of here." Shay stared straight ahead, unwilling to face the resolve she knew would be in his gaze. "I'm sure your brother is fine. This is all a big mistake."

When he said nothing, she finally looked his way and caught him watching her.

"Just being optimistic," she said.

"I'm a realist, and in this case, that means that I know Aiden is *not* fine. And we won't be either, until we find out who those men are and what they have to do with our missing plane and my missing brother."

* * *

Rick started up the Jeep, shifted into Reverse and edged back, watching for their pursuers. When the vehicle lurched forward onto what went for a road around these parts, he headed back. Time to return Shay to town.

Optimism.

He liked that about her, but she was just too inexperienced when it came to dealing with the reality of criminals in the world. He wished she hadn't come with him on this trip, but there had been no getting out of it. Aiden had said he needed a mechanic, and Shay was it.

They hadn't known what they'd face or that Aiden would disappear, and Rick still didn't know what was going on.

Guilt corded his throat as he pressed on the accelerator, pushing them back toward town. This road trip had been a waste of their time. "I know what I said about checking things out, but it's clearly not safe. I shouldn't have taken this road to begin with." Though he would have loved to see where this road led and knew he might not get another chance.

But neither could he risk Shay's safety. Aiden would have to wait. Aiden was an ex-marine, too, and knew how to take care of himself.

"It's not your fault, Rick," she said.

"I know what everyone thinks about my

brother," he said. "But I know him. This isn't like him. And those men…" Rick sighed. "Doesn't matter. I'm sending you back. The next flight out can't be too soon."

"No. I'm not going. If you're staying, you'll need someone to repair that plane. I'm your man."

It shouldn't have surprised him.

She hadn't wanted to make the trip to Alaska but she'd come anyway, saying that it was her job. She'd expressed her displeasure taking to the dirt road and the backcountry, but here she was, offering up her help in the face of difficult circumstances.

He'd had a certain image of her, working on the planes at Deep Horizon, handling everything they threw at her with grit and determination. The resolve she was showing now fit in with that picture…but he couldn't forget the fear in her voice earlier. She might be strong, might be tough, but she was still scared. It made him realize that in truth he didn't know much about her. Not really. And now she was either going to live up to the image he'd conjured in his head, or she wasn't. Likely, he would do the same for her. Live up to what she thought she knew about him or not.

As for Shay, he'd always had a feeling about her. And that was why he'd kept his distance.

Rick slowed the Jeep, the road growing narrow. Somehow, he had to convince her to go back.

"If we don't find Aiden, I'll need to get help. We'll worry about the plane later," he said.

Of course, it wasn't as if he could call 911 out here. They'd have to wait until they got back to true civilization—far from Tanaken's wilderness. Cell service pretty much followed the Alaska Highway system, but there were still long stretches of road that weren't covered, and anyone outside a major city was out of luck. Aiden had sprung for a satellite phone for this trek into the interior and since Rick had been simply meeting him in Tanaken, Rick hadn't thought he'd need one. He banged his palms against the steering wheel.

"And if he's not drunk somewhere and those men really have something to do with his disappearance, what do you think is going on?" Shay asked.

Rick knew of someone who'd been found dead—in Alaska, no less—recovering an airplane. That had been several years back. He hadn't thought of it until that moment. "I couldn't say."

Considering they were about as far from civilization as a person could get, anything in the world could have happened to Aiden.

A deep sense of dread lodged in his gut. He

had to find his brother. Couldn't leave him behind. Images of a raid in the desert accosted
him. He squeezed his eyes shut for an instant,
hating the unbidden memories. In the end, he'd
failed.

But never again.

Especially not this time, when it was his
brother who needed him.

Around the curve in the road, a fallen tree log
blocked their path. Rick jammed his foot against
the brake, sliding to a stop inches from the log.

"Rick!" Shay's scream sliced through the cab.

He jerked around to stare down headlights—
the truck plowing straight for them.

THREE

Bright lights—laser beams on the grill of the truck—loomed in Shay's vision, blinding her, growing larger as the truck raced toward the Jeep.

Her screams echoed in the cab, seeming to come from outside her body. She reached for the seat-belt clasp.

"We have to get out of here!" she yelled, struggling with the button. The seat belt kept her imprisoned, helpless against whoever in that truck wanted them dead.

To her right she glimpsed the ridge that dropped off only a few yards from her. She couldn't breathe. Her heart hammered against her ribs, demanding to be free, but her fingers were too slippery as she grappled with the clasp.

"Rick." Her desperate whisper cracked. "Who are these guys?"

Instead of answering her, Rick shifted into Reverse.

The truck roared forward, closing the distance too fast. Before Rick could back out of the way...

Impact!

Everything happened in slow motion.

The Jeep rocked with the collision, lurching to the side.

Oh, God, save us! Shay prayed as she felt her body thrown against the door, her head hitting the window, her screams filling the cab of the Jeep.

We're going to die!

When the initial crash was over, Shay gulped a breath.

The truck had just barely missed Rick's door, which would have completely pinned him behind the steering wheel. Behind his seat, the Jeep was crushed inward. The crash hadn't killed her and Rick, but pain, fear and shock kept her frozen in her seat. She tried to gather her wits and take in what was happening.

Through Rick's window, she could see into the cab of the other vehicle. She looked into dark, sinister eyes beneath an Alaska moose baseball cap, unable to grasp that the man driving the truck seemed to be enjoying this.

The truck pressed in on the Jeep; they were like two elks that had locked horns. The Jeep was moving, but not because Rick had put it in Drive. Instead, the tires ground against the dirt road as the truck pushed, and the Jeep slid sideways, gravity pulling it downward along the ridge. She squeezed Rick's shoulders. His door jammed shut, he moved toward her, climbing over the console, his intention clear—to get out of the Jeep and away from the truck.

The big-wheeled truck shoved the Jeep again, wheels spinning, throwing gravel and dirt. Shay peered out her window. "Rick?"

His expression was grim as he looked past her to see the ledge the Jeep was being pushed toward. They were powerless to stop what was happening. She'd never seen fear pour from his eyes like this. Slow and malicious, death awaited them at the bottom of the fall. Terror struck her heart at the thought of tumbling down the rocky precipice.

The Jeep edged them closer to the fall. "What are we going to do?" she asked. Desperation twisted her voice. She struggled, gasping for breath.

Rick slipped her seat belt off.

"What are you doing?" she asked.

"It's our only chance."

The right back tire breached the drop. "Hurry," she whimpered.

Weakness coursed through every limb in her shaking body.

"Hold on," Rick whispered in her ear. She heard a measure of reassurance in his voice but knew that was for her benefit only.

"Hold on to what? Rick, what are you thinking? Tell me so I'll know what I need to do."

She turned to stare at him, to look into his gray eyes that pierced her soul, his face millimeters from hers.

"Hold on to me." His gaze shifted to the window behind her.

She heard him swallow, an echo of her own horror. Did he really want her to hold on to him as they plummeted to their death? "Isn't there another way out?"

The right front tire slid over the edge and the Jeep shifted onto the forty-five-degree incline. They had fifty yards maybe before the incline took a complete two hundred-foot vertical drop.

Shay's breathing turned rapid. *Not now!*

She couldn't afford to hyperventilate now.

Behind Rick, she saw the truck's grille as it backed away. It had pushed them far enough and would leave gravity and momentum to do the rest.

"Rick." She gasped out his name. Hoping, praying for an answer.

"We're getting out," he said.

Shay could hardly believe him, but their options were limited.

Physics worked against them now, the tires slick against the gravelly incline even though the Jeep was parallel to the edge. They continued sliding, bouncing, and in fact picked up momentum.

"Now!"

Fast as lightning, Rick shoved her door open and wrapped his arms around her. She wasn't sure how he did it, but they tumbled from the vehicle milliseconds before it met with air and dropped over the final edge, the crashing noises resounding against the valley below. Greenery and gray sky flashed in her vision as branches stabbed and ripped at her body. She rolled with Rick, and yet somehow he protected her. Kept from crushing her.

Finally, they stopped rolling and her body crashed against Rick's. Air left her lungs. Blackness edged her vision. Strong arms squeezed her. She gasped for breath, listening to the Jeep as it continued to fall, smashing against the rocks.

Broken to smithereens.

A whimper broke from her throat. That could have been them if not for Rick. If not for his quick thinking. His ability to act on it and actually pull it off. And she still didn't know how they'd survived. Where had they fallen if not the bottom of the gorge? Looking around, she realized they'd landed on sort of a terrace of foliage before the drop-off.

"Rick," she said, and tried to move away, embarrassed at her pathetic moans.

"Shh," he whispered, and his arms tightened around her.

All her life, Shay had tried to hold her own. Didn't want to need anyone. But right now Shay couldn't help herself—she needed Rick at this moment. Needed his arms around her. Shay kept quiet and still, trusting the man that had saved their lives just now. She stared at the thicket where they'd fallen and suddenly realized why Rick wanted her silent.

She and Rick—they needed to be dead. She couldn't see through the greenery, which was good because that meant the men couldn't see her, either. But she heard them up on the ledge just above them. Doors slammed as their attackers climbed from their killing truck. What kind of people would do something like that? Shove two innocent people over the side of a cliff to their death? And why? Shay squeezed her eyes shut, but that didn't stop the awkward tears that streamed from the corners. She pressed her face into Rick's hard chest, fearing she might sob.

She needed to hold her breath, hold back the tears until the men were gone. Their voices echoed, but she couldn't make out the words.

Rick pressed his lips against the hair over her ear. "They need to think we're dead, understand?"

She nodded. Though she could barely hear the whisper on his warm breath, when she pressed her head against his chest again, she both heard and felt his pounding heart. Rick was scared, too.

Then she heard an unwelcome noise.

Shay stopped breathing, willing her heart to stop pounding.

One of the men slowly made his way down the incline. Would they keep searching until they found their bodies?

Rick held Shay to him, protecting her, protecting them both—if she moved or even made a sound, it would all be over.

The crunch of boots filled his ears. Someone cursed when he lost his footing. The scrape against the rocky slope told him when he'd gained traction again. What would the man see when he looked? Would seeing the demolished Jeep at the bottom of a cliff convince their pursuers that Rick and Shay were dead?

He squeezed his eyes shut, sending up a silent prayer. Images of his quick thinking—their only choice, the jump from the Jeep mere seconds from the moment it plummeted—played through his mind. He'd turned just in time so his body would take the impact as they rolled from the sliding Jeep. They were fortunate there had been thick underbrush to cushion their fall and to hide them afterward. They were fortunate the men hadn't climbed from their vehicle until it was all over. But was this the moment when their good fortune would run out?

Shay shifted against him, and he held her tight and still.

Quiet.

Admittedly, he was more than uncomfortable, his back partially against a flat boulder where he'd rolled. Branches within the thicket stabbed through his layered clothing to scrape his skin. Salty sweat beaded, despite the dropping temperature as evening approached, and trickled into the open wounds, making them burn.

Rick steadied his breathing. *Hold fast. Just a little longer.*

"Well?" Laced with edginess, a man's deep voice boomed from somewhere above them. "See anything?"

A few seconds passed, and they heard another curse—this one under someone's breath. And that someone was far too close.

Shay had done well to keep good and still for this long. But her slender form was beginning to tremble, if only a little.

He ran his hand over her soft hair and leaned in to whisper in her ear. "Just a little longer."

She stiffened and held her breath.

"Answer me." Again the voice boomed from somewhere above them.

Rick couldn't see a thing from where they lay, but that would keep them hidden, as well. An eagle screeched in the distant sky and a chilly gust rustled through the trees. Unbidden images of another time and place flashed through his mind and his heart rate soared.

A bomb exploded. The explosive gunfire from automatic weapons seared his thoughts.

Shay squeezed him, bringing him back to the moment. She inched her face up to look at him, the concern in her gaze clear. He could have lost it just then. Given them away.

All because of one fateful moment in his past. A moment he could never forget.

He gave a slight shake of his head. It wasn't as if he could explain that right now, if ever. But he sure didn't want those images to bother him at this moment when he had to maintain what little control he had over this situation.

"Nothing," the man said, his voice ringing mere yards from them. "There's nothing left. No way could anyone survive that."

"You'd better be sure. We can't let them make it to the claim."

"They're dead, all right? If by some miracle they survived that fall, how would they make their way out? Much less hike all the way to the mine."

At the words, Rick's pulse ratcheted up. The men had planned to kill them to prevent them from reaching the gold-mining claim? But why go to all that trouble? They were only interested in the plane, not the claim. Had they killed Aiden? He reined in the rage, the need to climb the ledge and pound the information out of these men. He was at a distinct disadvantage at the moment.

He released a sigh, then realized his mistake. Like Shay, he held his breath now. Just a little longer, he told himself.

He counted the seconds, praying the man hadn't heard his heavy exhale.

No way could anyone survive that. The words penetrated his chaotic thoughts—what reason did these men have for pursuing them, for attempting to kill them just to keep them from the camp? If it had anything at all to do with Aiden or even with Rick asking around the village for him, what chance did Aiden have?

He feared his brother was already dead.

No, God, please, no…. Rick wouldn't think that way. He could only hope that Aiden was in hiding, too, and hadn't had a chance to contact or warn them.

With Shay in his arms, her weight only a slight burden against him as he cushioned her on the ground, they listened as the man who'd been mere yards above them scraped and climbed his way back up to the road.

They released a collective sigh this time, and Rick didn't worry they'd be heard. But they weren't moving from this spot yet. Not until he knew for sure they were safe. Not until he heard the truck drive away, and even then he wouldn't leave the protective cover of foliage until he searched the area from their hiding place.

Conversation resumed above them and truck doors slammed. The rumble of the truck's engine started. Shay shifted to move from cover, but Rick held her tight. "Wait. We have to be sure," he whispered. She had to think he was being overly cautious, but she hadn't been through what he had.

Didn't know that things weren't always as they seemed.

Shay's trembling grew. She had to be in shock and was losing control, adrenaline fading as she began to believe the immediate threat was gone. Rick was grateful they'd escaped with their lives and, by all accounts, unscathed.

Of course, for him this was hardly anything

compared to what he'd already been through in his life. Now that the men were gone, he was more worried about another immediate threat—Shay. With her warmth and softness against him, a pang of tenderness shot through his heart, the kind of affection he remained guarded against at all times.

"Rick," she whispered. "Rick. You okay?"

He blinked, staring down at her big eyes looking up at him from where her head was pressed against his chest. He was supposed to be helping her, taking care of her. Protecting her. That was what men did. That was what soldiers did. But was he up to the challenge?

He wasn't a soldier now. He was just Rick Savage. Damaged goods.

The gentle concern in her eyes didn't help.

I'm dangerous to you.

FOUR

Of all the idiotic questions she could have asked. Of course he wasn't okay. Neither of them was okay. Someone had just tried to kill them.

She felt a few bruises springing up on her back and arms but knew that it could have been so much worse. And maybe it was worse than she realized—something in his eyes, the way he looked at her right now, scared her. He was wearing that same wild and distant gaze she'd seen before, as though his mind had dragged him to a place that was anywhere but here and now.

Shay didn't like it. Nor did she like that her hands were shaking. Her whole body trembled, and if it weren't for Rick holding her against him, she'd probably lose control completely.

Her mind wandered as well, taking her back to the day when she'd last seen that look in his eye—the day when he'd aimed a weapon at her head. She'd startled him taking a nap in the office and she'd found herself looking down the muzzle of a gun. After seeing the darkness that tortured him, she knew she'd been right to keep her resolve not to give in to her attraction to him. She couldn't fall in love. It was too risky, especially with this man.

The guy had issues.

Something bad must have happened to him during his military service. But Rick kept it all hidden inside. Even if she were prepared to fall for someone, she couldn't handle another man in her life who kept it all inside. Who didn't open up. Her father had hurt her enough. It wasn't worth the risk.

She closed her eyes, remembering how Rick's hands had gripped her and, in the span of a heartbeat, yanked her from the sliding box of death, his body cushioning her as they fell, branches and bushes breaking their fall.

Rick had saved her. He'd saved them both. In light of that fact, Shay shoved aside the shadows she'd seen behind his eyes—shadows that had nothing at all to do with their current predicament.

Their current predicament was enough.

With his arms wrapped around her, she could almost forget her aches and bruises. But she was still dazed from their near miss with death

know that we need to get out of here. Find a way up to the road and get back to the village. Even if we're safe from those men, the weather could turn on us, and the night will be cold. In the thirties, at least."

He shoved from their hiding place on the small terrace of greenery before the rocky drop. Shay followed cautiously, careful not to step too close to the drop-off where the Jeep had met its final demise.

Looking up at the edge from where they'd fallen, Shay shook her head in disbelief.

How...how did we survive that? The trembling started up her legs again. To think they'd rolled from the Jeep and...Rick had taken the brunt of that fall, protecting her more than she could have imagined.

His back to her now, she took in his broad shoulders and noted a few rips in his sweatshirt, all the way through the shirt underneath. He had to be in pain, yet he hadn't said a word. Shay took a step toward him and lifted her hand wanting to touch his back, but she quickly withdrew. Unwilling for him to see her shaking again, she wrapped her arms around herself.

Rick gazed up the ledge that led back to the road. "I don't think we can make it back up from here. The top of the ledge is just out of my reach.

There's nothing for me to grab onto, even if I was a rock climber—which I'm not."

Neither was she. Shay's heart sank. "What are we going to do?"

"We'll have to find a different way." He scratched his jaw and turned his attention to the valley below.

Glad she'd dressed in layers, Shay rubbed her arms, this time from the chill in the air. "Even if we could have made the road, we need our coats, don't we?"

"Yeah, and we need our gear. The weather could turn ugly. And if that's not enough, the guy I paid to rent his Jeep for the day isn't going to be happy. Come on." He held his palm open. "We're getting out of here."

When Shay hesitated, he frowned. "What? Don't you trust me?"

There was a question she was sure he didn't want answered. The truth was, she could only trust him so far. "It's not that," she hedged.

Rick withdrew his hand and waited. A stiff breeze wrapped around her.

"Then what is it? We need to hurry."

How did she tell him? She looked at the valley, at the drop where the Jeep had landed. "I don't know if I can."

He shifted his weight, his gaze skimming the gorge and the valley beyond. Understanding dawned on his face. "Sure you can. We'll make our way around and descend along the slow decline. I'll be right there with you every step of the way."

"Rick, just standing here like this, everything is spinning. If I look around…"

His forehead crinkled. "You're not telling me you're afraid of heights, are you?"

The words hung in her throat, so she nodded.

He studied Shay, her cute short crop hugging features that still looked pretty despite the smudges and the scratch from their crash through the underbrush. They'd barely escaped with their lives, so he should be grateful a few scratches was the most she had, but it wasn't over yet.

How was it that an airplane mechanic was afraid of heights?

Now, that was a story he wanted to hear.

That could also explain much of her stiffness during their travel to Alaska. He'd been a little suspicious, but she'd claimed she just wasn't happy about having to make the trip. He could relate to that.

He scratched his chin and flattened the smile that threatened. "I thought you looked a little sick on the flight to Fairbanks. I just figured it was motion sickness." Rick stepped closer.

"Well, now you know. I'm afraid of heights. Afraid of flying. Not so uncommon." Shay's big purplish-blue eyes stared up at him again. He recalled when she'd done that moments before—looked up at him. He'd held her in his arms then....

Color rose in her cheeks. Was that from the dipping temperatures or something else?

His emotional wall flew up—he had to guard himself, keep from feeling anything for this woman. Even if he were free to fall for her, which he wasn't, this sure wasn't the time.

But seeing her like this, this small vulnerability in her tough act, hitched a little place in his heart.

"Yep. Now I know. But you have to realize that if we're going to survive this, we need to get moving."

Shay shrugged, looking resigned to the situation. But that wasn't good enough for Rick. He was counting on her to make this work—both their lives depended on it.

"Listen, I've got your back, okay? You don't need to worry about falling."

She didn't appear reassured.

"Is there something else? Something you're not telling me?" What was she hiding? What happened when someone was afraid of heights? Did they pass out? *Oh, Lord, please, no.* Then again, maybe carrying her dead weight would be faster than assisting her down.

"Shay." He kept talking because she wouldn't respond. "You can do this. You're strong, and you're tough. We all have our weaknesses, so this is yours. No big. Just don't look down."

"I'm sorry, I'm still trying to wrap my head around this whole thing." She took in a deep breath. "You're right. Let's do it."

Good girl. Rick held his hand out again. "I promise I won't tell anyone about your…um… condition."

The corner of her mouth lifted and she smacked him on the arm.

"Ow." He grabbed his arm, pretending it hurt.

Shay moved by him without taking his hand.

He grabbed her arm. "There's a slope here and then some boulders and a drop-off. I think it levels off after a while, but let me help you to get your footing, okay?"

"Once we're in the trees and can't see how high we are, I'll be good." Still, Shay placed her hand in his and together they maneuvered the incline, which was a little steeper than he'd anticipated.

Slipping, Shay yelped.

Rick held tight, his muscles tensing to keep himself steady on his feet along with Shay. "I've got you."

When they made it to the boulders, Rick stopped. "Let me climb down first to find the best way."

Shay nodded.

"So how did you end up becoming an aviation mechanic?"

Asking her a few questions might keep her mind off worrying about what lay ahead. His mind, too. He wasn't scared of heights, but that didn't mean he felt at ease. No matter how you looked at things, making their way back to the road would be a difficult task. But Rick couldn't just sit around and wait for a rescue that might not come for days, if that. No one was expecting them back anytime soon.

"Do you really want to know?" Shay's soft voice bounced off the boulders as he made his way down.

"Yes, I do. And I think it's okay for you to start down. It's an easy descent—just watch your footing."

His breathing was a little harder than he'd have liked. This shouldn't be anything like a tough workout—he thought he was in better shape than this. Maybe it was the altitude. He glanced up to see Shay making her way down. Fortunately, the trees were thick here and she shouldn't see anything to set off her fear of heights. He hoped.

"My father was a mechanic. I watched him work, helped him and learned from him while I was growing up."

Rick already knew that answer, of course. He'd heard the other guys talking about her. But he wanted to hear it from her. Get her talking.

"And you liked it so much that you decided to follow in his footsteps." Rick climbed across the flat top of a big boulder, beginning to see that he'd made a mistake.

"Yep. That's about it."

He paused at the edge, confirming the drop would be too much for him to jump. He couldn't safely hit the rocks below without risking serious injury. Shay definitely couldn't do this.

"Okay, hold up right where you are." He directed his voice in her direction, but he'd lost sight of her.

A small animal scurried through the underbrush below. The earthy scent of spruce and untainted wilderness enveloped him. They were really in the thick of it now.

"Rick? Where are you?"

"I'm just on the other side of these rocks. You'll see me in a minute. I have to find another way down."

"It's getting colder."

Too bad they couldn't have done this retrieval in the summer.

"When we get down to the Jeep and get our coats, I'll make a fire and we'll rest for a while."

Rick hated that they had to start this adventure already in need of rest after two long days of travel. But sometimes you just had to gut it up. He prayed they found their coats. Everything could have fallen out at different places along the Jeep's tumble. Stuff could be sprawled all over the valley, never to be found again.

Besides their coats, his main concern was finding his gun.

He needed that gun. They could face wild animals, but mostly he feared they might face the two-legged kind, and they weren't turning out to be too friendly in these parts. Rick wished now that he'd used the weapon at that instant when the truck had plowed toward them. He could have taken aim and taken out the driver. Maybe. It had all happened so fast.

That might not have stopped the vehicle from barreling toward them. In that split second, he'd made a decision to drive the Jeep out of harm's way. That decision had been a mistake. Too bad he was no stranger to those kinds of mistakes.

But right now focusing on his failures wouldn't help Shay. Rick scrambled along the boulders, searching for a better way down. Concentrating on the task at hand instead of trying to make conversation with Shay was probably a good idea, as well.

He glanced up and spotted her watching him. "I think you're good to follow me now." He left out that talking too much had distracted him and led them on the wrong path.

Shay nodded, seeming content to end their conversation for now. He might ask about her family if they had a chance to rest. And there was her reference about something happening and her father teaching her to shoot. He'd like to know what that was all about, if she was willing to share.

Rick's foot slipped on a boulder.

He grasped at the rock, but he couldn't get a handhold on the surface.

Despite his best efforts, his body slid and he fell backward through the air, Shay screaming somewhere in the distance.

FIVE

Oh, my. Oh, my gosh... .

Panic wrapped a tight cord around her throat.
She gasped for breath, and finally sucking it in,
she screamed. "Rick!"

But he didn't answer.

Shay called again. "Rick! Are you okay?"

Without thinking about her footing, she made
her way down the rocks. She had to get to him.
"Rick, please answer me."

*Oh, Lord, please let him be okay. Let this be
some kind of joke.* But she didn't think he would
joke about something like that, especially at a
time like this. Shay chided herself. How many
times had she been invited to go rock climbing?
To go skating or jogging or to a workout class?
She spent too much time cooped up in a ware-
house just doing her job. Maybe if she had ac-
cepted those invitations, she'd have a better idea
of what to do now. She'd be better equipped to
climb down these rocks. She'd be in much bet-

ter physical condition, too. She didn't know how to do anything other than work. And now she was paying for that.

When Shay made it to the point where she'd last seen Rick, she crawled on shaky hands and knees to the edge and peered over.

"Rick?" She injected a little hope into her tone.

There he lay, at the bottom of the pile of rocks. "Oh, no...."

Careful not to make the same mistake he'd made, she backtracked and made her way around the mountain of smooth and jagged rocks. "Rick Savage, don't you leave me here alone."

Talk. Just keep talking. He'll hear you and be all right by the time you make it down. "Can you hear me, Rick?"

Shay found herself staring at a drop of about five feet. Not that far, really, but if she didn't land just right, she might not be much better off than Rick. Or worse, she could be injured and in pain and with no way to get help.

Shay slid her gaze to all possible ways down, but there was nothing for it. She pressed flat on the rounded boulder and slid her body against it as far as she could.

She pulled in a breath. *Please, God, let me land right.*

Releasing her slight grip, she allowed herself to slide and then drop.

Her feet hit the ground and she plopped back on her backside. So far so good. Still, she had a stretch to go to make it all the way down to Rick. He hadn't responded to anything she'd said. And *that* wasn't so good.

Fear like she'd never known—even when the killer truck had shoved them from the road—coursed through her. At least she'd been with Rick at that moment, and with that, she realized that despite the uneasiness she felt at the shadows in his eyes, she'd felt safe as long as he'd been there.

What if Rick never woke up?

No. She couldn't think that way. Careful to make her way to him cautiously and safely, she nevertheless hurried down the rest of the pile of rocks. Though descending hadn't been that easy, the stack of rocks had given them a path to the base of the mountain and into the gorge.

Her feet firmly planted on earth carpeted in pine needles, Shay rushed around the edges of the rock pile. "Rick," she gasped, running.

There. He lay sprawled on his back. Motionless.

She fell to her knees next to him, wanting to touch him, jar him awake, but fearing she might hurt him more, depending on his injuries.

"Where are you hurt?" she asked, knowing he wouldn't answer. She ran her hands down his arms and legs, gently patting to make sure there wasn't an obvious break.

Then she rested her palms on his head and pressed her face near his. "Now, you listen to me, Rick Savage. I need you. Please wake up. I have no idea what to do without you."

Her palms resting against his stubble-roughened cheeks, she felt the rush of warmth through her hands and up her arms. She'd had a thing for this man for the longest time, in spite of the gun incident. Seeing him like this sent shards of pain slicing through her core. "Please, please wake up."

Brushing his dark hair from his forehead, she noted the sun-bleached strands, remnants of a summer spent outdoors. She ran her hands all the way through the thickness. "I've always wanted to do that...." She murmured the words to herself.

"If only you were awake, then I wouldn't have to feel guilty for doing that without your permission." She sat back on her rear, thinking. Praying.

"If you don't wake up, what in the world am I going to do? Where would I begin to get you help? The sky's growing dark. I wanted to make it to the Jeep for our coats before making a fire, but maybe I should just make one here and wait for you to wake up. That's something I can do, at least."

Shay rubbed her arms, warming them against the cold. She had to make a decision. It might already be too late either way. "Maybe I should just leave you and find the Jeep myself so I can bring back our coats and anything else I can find. How far could it be from here anyway?"

A vise squeezed her heart. How could she save Rick?

"Maybe if you were a jerk, it might be easier to leave you. But no, you have to be cute and…" Shay sighed. "Cute and nice."

There, she'd said it.

Rick groaned and slapped a hand to his head. "Did anyone ever tell you that you talk too much?"

"You're…you're awake. Oh, thank You, God." Shay pressed her hands over her mouth. But how much had he heard? "And no. No one has ever told me I talk too much."

Tears burned behind her eyes.

Rick sat up, rubbing his head, his hair a scruffy mess. He blinked a few times, then pinned her with his grays. "You're a sight for sore eyes."

"Me?"

"Yeah. You made it down all by your lonesome." Rick sat up, then pushed up to stand, a little unsteady on his feet. "I'm sorry to scare you like that."

"Never mind about that." Shay stood, too. "Are you okay? You think you have a concussion?"

Rick rubbed his face and then his neck. "Nah. I'm good to go. We need to make up for lost time."

Shay started to move by him, though she didn't know where she was going. But the way he looked at her left her wondering just how much he'd heard. What an idiot she'd been to flap her trap like that, but talking kept her company, chased the fear away.

He stepped in her path, standing a little too near for comfort. "I'm glad you don't think I'm a jerk."

And just a little too glad that you think I'm cute. Too glad for my own good.

When Shay's eyes widened, he knew she wondered what else he'd heard. Though he'd been unconscious for a short while and had a dull throbbing ache to show for it, he'd felt himself coming to and heard an ongoing conversation Shay was having with herself and him. Her soft, caring voice had brought him back from the darkness.

The problem was he couldn't stop thinking

about her words and he had no business thinking about them now, in this situation. Or ever.

"Let's get moving." Rick tore his gaze from the heat of surprise in hers and focused on surviving. "Stay close to me."

After getting his bearings again, he headed due north in the direction where the Jeep should be. Evergreens and lush undergrowth had taken over the gulch they'd descended into, and maybe somewhere at the bottom they'd find a river or stream.

He shoved through the thick scrub, trying to make time while they still had the last of daylight to guide their path. The temperatures had long ago started dropping below comfort level. If they didn't recover their coats and make a fire soon, they were done for. The full brunt of winter wasn't on them yet; still, the temperatures could vary from extreme cold to extreme heat during the spring and fall months. Today had been a relatively warm day, but he had a feeling that warmth was on its way out if the temperatures so far were any indication.

Behind him, Shay was breathing hard, and he wasn't doing much better.

He paused and turned to face her. "You okay?"

"Sure," she said, a shiver to her words. "Keep moving."

Of course she understood the danger they'd

face if they didn't find what they were lookin
for. They hiked on for a few more minutes, darl
ness finally closing in on them.

"How much farther, Rick?" Her teeth chattere
a little. "You sure we're headed the right way?

"It has to be around here somewhere. I knov
this is the place."

Rick gazed up where the moon shone abov
them, illuminating a familiar cliff, but he hadn
exactly seen this side of it from the top, makin
it hard to gauge their position. "Recognize that?

"You mean the ledge of death?"

"Is that what we're calling it?" He almos
chuckled at the name she'd given it.

"No. That's what we're going to call it if w
end up dying because we can't find the Jeep."

"We're not going to die. We'll build a fire an
stay warm tonight, then look for the Jeep tomo
row if we have to. But for now, stay close. Let'
work our way over and hope to find the Jeep
If Providence is on our side, we might even b
able to turn on the lights."

Shay huffed. "I know my stuff, but that doesn
mean I could get that thing running again."

Forcing his way through the brush in the ligh
of the moon with Shay remaining near, Ricl
smiled to himself. "I bet you could get it to star
even if it sank in the river."

"Flattery will get you nowhere, Mr. Savage."

Mr. Savage. He liked the sound of her voice when she said it. What an idiot. Now he was a jerk for thinking along those lines. Shay didn't deserve damaged goods.

When Rick took another step forward, he kicked something that had a metallic ring to it. They both froze.

Clouds had momentarily slipped over the moon, leaving them in darkness. He leaned over and pressed his hand against the cold metal, sliding it until he came to the end. "The bumper. Or one of them. It must have come off."

"We're close, then." Shay's voice rang with hope.

"Yeah, close." Faced with the prospect of finding everything they needed with only intermittent moonlight to guide them and the cold grip of an Alaskan night threatening them, Rick started to think maybe they'd made a mistake. This wasn't going to work. "Wait here."

"No. I'm coming with you."

He slipped his hand into hers and squeezed. She didn't try to pull away as he led her in search of the body of the vehicle. He hoped everything they needed remained intact inside what was left of the vehicle.

As they pushed through a thick stand of

bushes, Shay's gasp reflected his own morbid thoughts. The Jeep rested overturned and on its side, the front end and right side collapsed. Shay had been sitting on the passenger's side. Now that seat no longer existed, having been crushed by the toppling two-ton vehicle.

They should have been ecstatic to find it—at least in the face of their circumstances—but instead, Rick and Shay both stared in shock. The next thing Rick knew, Shay was in his arms, trembling. When had he tugged her to him? Or had she simply stepped against him and wrapped her arms around him?

He shook his thoughts free. "This time I need you to stay here. I'm going to shove it over so it won't be unstable, and then we can search inside, okay?"

She nodded her agreement, taking a few steps back. "Be careful."

Rick marched around the Jeep, watching where he stepped so he wouldn't twist his ankle or stumble. He wasn't exactly sure he could right the thing, but it appeared to rest at an awkward angle, looking as though even the slightest nudge would push it completely over. The sound of pebbles trickling down the cliff face drew his attention up, though he couldn't see much. H hoped any rocks loosened by the Jeep's tumble didn't decide to slide while he stood here.

"Shay? You out of the way?" he called.

"I'm good. Go ahead."

Rick pressed his foot against the crumpled roof and shoved. Hard.

The Jeep rocked back and forth, the sound of twisting metal resounding through the gorge. Okay. This would take a little more than a mere shove on his part. He pressed his back against the roof and heaved with all his strength. While the Jeep teetered, Rick stepped back and kicked it hard.

It toppled onto the tires, and the driver's-side door, already dented from the first collision, fell off, clanking through the night. Dust rose while steam spewed from the radiator. Rick's shoulders rocked with an incredulous laugh that the radiator was only just now ejecting its contents.

Shay jogged up to him, her cloudy breath visible in the moon's illumination. "The door light went on a little. You see that?"

She grinned. Funny how such a small thing in the worst of circumstances could bring a smile to her lips.

He'd always liked her smile. "Yeah, I see it," he said, but he wasn't talking about the light that had come on when the door had fallen off.

Then her attention shifted away from him, a look of alarm spreading over her face as she angled her head, listening.

Somewhere in the distance, an ominous sound echoed.

SIX

What was that?

Unmoving, Shay stood in the night, listening. Next to her, Rick did the same. A few seconds passed, but it seemed more like an eternity as Shay strained to hear the noise again. But she heard nothing except the trickle of a stream a few yards away.

And that noise still rang in her mind.

Rick exhaled. "Let's stay quiet, just in case."

"Just in case what?" She kept her question to a whisper. "Those men aren't coming back, are they? You aren't planning to head to the mine now, are you?" She knew Rick was still worried about his brother, as was she, but surely he planned to go back to town and regroup before going out to find Aiden again. Clearly it would take more than the two of them to figure this out.

"Shh." Rick gave her a funny look. "You're not helping."

What was the noise they'd heard? Mountain lion? Or the whine of an ATV? If she could hear it again, maybe she could tell.

Rick said nothing as he crawled carefully into the Jeep. Shay wanted to help and moved to the other side, but she could hardly get through the mangled metal that used to be the passenger side. She peered through the small opening that was left. Rick wasn't looking for their coats—that was obvious—so Shay made her way to the back.

The hatch was gnarled and bent, and she doubted she could get it open from this side. The sliver of moonlight, along with the small door light that flickered on and off, afforded Shay enough illumination to spot a blanket and their coats.

"Rick, I see them," she said. "Can I get a little help here?"

He eyed her from the driver's side, then squeezed between the seats. He grunted as he crawled through the mangled vehicle to the backseat. He searched all the crevices and every inch of the floorboard that he could reach but never looked over the backseat.

"What are you looking for? Didn't you hear me?" she asked. "The coats are back here."

In the moonlight, she could see that he had that look on his face again.

Then she realized—he was looking for his gun.

She didn't say anything. She didn't want to think about it. Didn't want to remember that day he'd aimed a gun at her, but the images accosted her anyway. She squeezed her eyes shut, hating the memory that swept over her.

On that evening several months ago, Rick had crashed on the leather sofa in the Deep Horizon office, and Shay had been the last one out. She didn't know if he planned to sleep there or what. Maybe she shouldn't have tried to wake him, but she nudged him in case he hadn't intended to fall asleep at the office.

In a flash he was on his feet, aiming his weapon at her as if she'd come to kill him. As if he was only defending himself. It took her a few seconds to coax him from his startled daze. To convince him of who she was. And the fear of that moment had tapped back to another fateful day years ago, a day Rick knew nothing about but that she could never forget.

As Shay pushed the thoughts away, her legs trembled from more than the frigid temperatures.

"Here you go." Rick wrapped the coat around her.

When had he climbed from the Jeep? The forbidding thoughts had temporarily imprisoned her, keeping her from noticing.

She slipped her arms into the coat. "Did you find it?"

"Find what?"

"Your gun."

"No, but I'm going to make a fire first, and then I'll look some more." He shrugged into his own jacket.

"Aren't you afraid we'll signal to someone that we're here?"

He eyed her. "You have to view it in terms of risk versus benefit. We could die without that fire, depending on how low the temps dip tonight. This is Alaska. I doubt anyone will be out in the middle of a cold Alaskan night looking for two people they already believe dead."

Shay didn't add what else the guy had said— even if they survived, how could they make it out? They sure hadn't come prepared to survive the night or a hike out.

Shay blew out a breath. "Why don't you let me build a fire while you look?"

Rick paused and stared at her hard and long.

"What? Can't a girl know how to build a fire?"

He grinned and stuck his hand into a pack he'd tugged from the Jeep. "Go ahead, if you're up for it."

Shay caught the water bottle he tossed her. "There anything else in there?"

"You mean like something to start a fire with besides two sticks?" He chuckled and dug around in the bag. "I didn't bring this, by the way. Was already in the back. I saw it when I stashed our stuff."

He tossed her a plastic bag holding a couple of lighters and some other stuff. Must be a home-made survival kit.

"Actually, I was thinking about food," she said. "Is there anything to eat in there?"

"I'm looking."

"On the fire, I wasn't joking. I can do it. Another thing my dad taught me."

Along with how to aim and shoot a weapon. And to be self-sufficient.

"Good man, your dad. Never know when something like that is going to come in handy."

"You mean like now."

"Yep. Like now. And you never know when something like this—" he held up a buck knife "—is going to come in handy."

Holding the few supplies they'd found, Shay backed away from the Jeep.

"Let's do the fire together," he said, and continued to forage around in the gnarled vehicle. "We need to find the best place, gather kindling and fuel. Together we can make better time. And to help power you through it, here you go."

He held something out to her.

Sustenance.

Shay reached for the nutrition bar, but he didn't release it. When Shay looked up at him, he held her gaze. "You did good today, Shay."

Heat warmed her insides and crawled up her neck. A compliment from him shouldn't have been such a big deal. "I should be saying that to you. You're the one who saved us both from the fall. Thank you for what you did. For saving my life."

"You know that we're not out of it yet. Maybe you should hold on to those words and hopefully you can thank me later. Or maybe I'll thank you later. You might have to return the favor at some point."

Shivers crawled up her spine at his reminder of their predicament. *I hope not.*

"Is it even possible for us to make it back to Tanaken without those men discovering that we survived?" Somehow Shay didn't imagine that was likely.

"Once we make it through the night, that'll be our next goal. Make it back up to the road. Somehow. We can't make it to the village without that road, but we'll stay hidden if we hear a vehicle until we determine it's safe."

"Then what?"

"Hopefully I can get help from the local authorities to figure out who attacked us and find Aiden. Find out why someone attempted to murder us to keep us away from a mining claim. I'll call Connor to help, too, of course. And you, Shay, you're going back to Fairbanks, if not all the way home. The plane isn't worth it anymore."

Near the banks of the stream, they found a bare patch of ground.

"Okay, this looks good, but..." Rick paused.

"But what?"

"Shh. I'm listening."

Shay tensed, understanding he feared being discovered. If only they didn't need the warmth of a fire.

"I'm going to walk the perimeter, just to be sure there's no one around. Okay?"

"You saying you want me to stay here? Alone?"

"I'll be quicker and quieter if I do this myself. You'll be fine. Just sit against that tree trunk over there. I won't be long."

Then Rick disappeared into the night.

Shay tried to shove away the fear as darkness surrounded her, closing in. The old fallen birch Rick had indicated lay a few feet away. Shay leaned against the trunk, but she remained stiff and alert to danger while she waited on Rick.

Whether or not they could find a way out of the gorge remained to be seen, but she kept her spirits high with the reminder that they'd found food and water. If they couldn't find a way out, maybe the Jeep could serve as a modicum of shelter if they needed to wait it out for a rescue that wouldn't come for days. Shay sighed. So much for her efforts to think positive. Some optimist she was.

Shimmering colors splayed across the night sky—what she could see of it down in the gorge—and seemed to belie her morbid thoughts. Shay gasped and sat up, taking in the northern lights. She'd never seen the aurora borealis except in pictures. How she wished they weren't down in this gulch so she could watch the display across the whole sky. Where was Rick? Was he watching, too?

She heard footfalls in the brush and stiffened, but Rick's form soon appeared. True to his words, he'd returned in only a few moments, and his arms were filled with kindling and wood. "Okay, I didn't see or hear anything suspicious. I think we're good to build that fire. Let's pray I'm right."

With those words he knelt down, and while he positioned the kindling, he also prayed. Tha took Shay by surprise—she hadn't thought he'd meant what he'd said literally—but it was a welcome surprise. Shay listened to this man as he prayed, revealing a quiet but strong faith. His prayer for God to lead them through this, to be with them, touched her in a deep place in her heart.

The kindling positioned, she was the one to coax the flame from the lighter into a small but adequate campfire. Enough to keep them alive through the night. With her coat on and the blanket, the fire thawed her cold extremities and re-heated her core enough that she could almost fall asleep, especially knowing that Rick was there.

Shay sat against the log, getting as comfortable as could be expected, preparing to spend the next few hours resting before their hike back to the village. Resting—and praying they could stay hidden and out of sight long enough to make it back to town.

Rick stood near the fire, holding a stick into the yellow flames, the reflection dancing in his eyes. He looked vigilant to their surroundings. He wanted to keep them safe, and Shay appreciated his efforts, but she couldn't help but wonder what he was thinking.

The moment when the men shoved them toward the ledge played across her mind, as it had almost constantly since it happened. "I've been trying to figure things out. What do you think, Rick? Why did those men try to kill us?"

"Try, Shay? They *think* they successfully killed us. We've been over this already anyway. I'm no closer to an answer now than I was before."

"Come on, Rick. We've been dancing around this conversation all afternoon. I think I deserve the truth. You don't have to protect me."

"I'm not keeping information from you. You know as much as I do. They followed us to kill us. Somehow the mining claim is involved, and I can't imagine that it's unrelated to Aiden." Rick's face contorted, revealing his pain, and then he looked away.

Shay knew he was trying to be strong for her, but in moments when he thought she wasn't looking, like now, she'd caught the apprehension etched across his features. She wanted to get to her feet and reach for him, comfort him. Let him know it was going to be all right.

They could even comfort each other. Except saying that it would be all right would be a lie. There wasn't anything she could do or honestly say to make things better. That men would kill them because of Aiden had to mean the absolute worst for Rick's brother.

And the question still remained… "Why would anyone want to harm Aiden or go out of their way to try to murder us over a stupid plane? Without repairs, it's not like he could even take the plane."

He shook his head slightly, staring into the flames. "There's obviously something much bigger going on. But it doesn't really matter. We're not in a very good place to do anything about it."

Shay sighed. Even if she could convince herself to go to him, that it was the right thing to do, she didn't have the energy.

"Shouldn't you sit down for a while since we have a lot of hiking to do?" *Come sit next to me. Keep me warm.*

"Yeah, sure. In a minute."

She hid her disappointment at his answer. Odd how she felt about him. She was still wary of him, yet there were so many other emotions she was struggling with, as well. He was the man to get them through this. No doubt there. She was attracted to him; no doubt there, either. He was strong, kind and gentle—qualities she already knew about but had never experienced from Rick in quite this way before. And the fact that he was a man of faith… She'd known he was a Christian, but seeing him in action, hearing his words, made something shift in her heart.

It was like a tug-of-war, a battle she shouldn't even have been fighting.

She could never let herself act on those feelings. Loving someone was too risky, too painful. And even if she wasn't afraid to love, there was a hazardous side to Rick. He couldn't be trusted.

He was dangerous.

But right now this dangerous man was the one she had to trust with her life.

Watching the fire consuming the wood he'd gathered, transforming it into glowing embers, could mesmerize Rick if he let it. He wished he could give in to it, but his senses were on high alert in case they were discovered. His mind ticked through the list of things they'd need to do to get out of here.

He hated they'd had to make a fire that could signal anyone with mal intent looking for them, but freezing to death was a greater risk to them at the moment. They had to warm up, get some rest then be on their way. Those killers thought he and Shay were dead, so maybe they'd catch a break and no one would be looking for any signs of life from them, like a fire.

He felt Shay watching him. He tried to hide his anxiety about their circumstances. Getting back to town would have been a challenge even if they'd simply broken down on the side of the undeveloped road. But down in this gorge, just getting back to the road might be a notch above his skill and pay level. He certainly hadn't bargained for any of this, but neither had any of them. And Shay. She understood just how dire their circumstances were.

They needed much more than their coats and a protein bar to survive this. The weather could turn seriously ugly without any notice. And even if the weather cooperated, it could still take days to get out of this gorge and back to Tanaken.

Days.

Rick let that sink in. He didn't know if they could last that long.

Finally, he allowed himself to drop next to Shay and sit against the log. Eye level with the fire, he felt the warmth more now, or maybe that was the heat emanating from Shay. He felt her presence keenly but kept his thoughts focused on their problems. Rubbing his temples, he realized he was letting too much of his apprehension show. Fortunately, Shay didn't seem to notice, but stared into the fire. In his peripheral vision, he saw the flames flickering across her face, highlighting the same exhaustion he felt.

Add to everything, he still hadn't found the gun. He needed that gun. He could think of too many situations where that gun would come in handy, not even counting for protection. It wouldn't do much against a Kodiak bear or an Alaskan grizzly, but it was something.

The blaze crackled and sizzled, and just for

a moment, Rick allowed himself to rest and let the flames entrance him. From the corner of his eye, he saw Shay yawn. His gaze drifted over to her, cataloging all her contradictions. If he saw her on the street, he'd never guess her chosen career and that she'd been hailed one of the best. She was of medium build, athletic and strong, but her face, her mannerisms and her actions, now that he'd gotten to know her a little better, were decidedly feminine—something she hid from them all back at the Deep Horizon hangar. There she'd never let down her guard or let anyone see her vulnerabilities.

A situation like this could strip away a person's well-crafted barriers. Rick himself was feeling like a battering ram was pounding against the walls of his heart. Not just where Shay was concerned, but for his brother, too. He couldn't stand to think that his brother might be dead, but if he had somehow survived, where was he? Was he held captive at the mining camp? Had he been beaten or harmed?

Rick's gut churned at the thought.

He shoved to his feet, startling Shay. "I'm going to look for the gun."

She frowned.

"You'll be fine. I'm just over there. It couldn't have fallen far."

"What about the noise we heard earlier? You

never said what you thought it might be." Her eyes glowed in the firelight and she chewed on her bottom lip, looking so nervous that he wanted to reach out and comfort her. Another time and another place. If Rick were a different person.

Rick looked away. Why did he have to start thinking about her like this?

"I didn't say, because I don't know." *But that was just one reason why I need to find the gun.*

He knew his answer didn't sound convincing, but he honestly didn't have a better one. He truly didn't know what they'd heard. For a moment, he'd even thought he'd heard voices, but it could have been anything at all echoing through the gorge. If they hadn't just escaped being killed, he might have called out to see if anyone answered. Making it back to Tanaken without running into anyone who might try to kill them was his priority.

He slid her one last glance, then trudged away from the firelight.

"Please hurry," she said under her breath, so low she probably didn't think he'd heard.

I promise... He bit the words back. What was he doing thinking of making promises?

Rick eyed the cliff side. The moon had shifted and wasn't illuminating much at the moment. Worst case, he'd have to wait until the sun shed some light in the gorge. But even if he didn't find it until then, he at least had to start looking now. Making his way to the Jeep only a few yards from Shay, he stayed hidden in the brush but watched her, searching the area for any signs of danger. He needed that weapon.

In an ever-widening spiral, he searched the ground. After half an hour, he wanted to give up. His gun had been resting on the seat between the two of them in the Jeep. It could easily have fallen out of the vehicle with them when they'd jumped.

And in that case, he should have looked near where they'd fallen. Rick raked a hand through his hair, feeling like the idiot that he was. But it wouldn't do them any good to think like that.

Maybe it had fallen next to the door on the passenger side and was wrapped in that tangle of metal. What hope did he have of retrieving it if it was? And if he found it there, it probably wouldn't be intact and functional.

He ran a hand over his scruffy jaw. He had to try. He couldn't just sit by the fire and do nothing. If he sat down again, he might not get up for hours, and one of those feelings was all over him again, telling him they had to get moving.

For all he knew, those murderers would come back to hide the Jeep. Hide the evidence. Hide the bodies. Why hadn't he considered that sooner?

Time was shorter than he'd thought.

Back at the Jeep, the door light was still shining. Batteries usually died when you needed them the most, so he wasn't counting on it working much longer, but at least he had it for now. Rick would be thankful for small things. He climbed back into the ravaged vehicle and tried not to think about what their bodies would have looked like if they'd been trapped inside. The passenger side was all scrunched up against the driver's side, but he thrust his hand through an opening in the mangle and twist of the door, window, frame and seat. He felt around but couldn't make out much. Would he even know the gun's metal when he felt it?

Yes.

He'd feel the custom tactical grip glove he'd put on it. He'd thought it would give him more control. As if it were only the weapon he needed more control over. He needed control over much more than that. Tugging his hand free, he released a pent-up breath. He'd opened the door so he and Shay could slip out.

Please don't let that gun be at the top of the cliff where they'd fallen.

This was a hopeless search without sunlight, and he'd already left Shay too long.

A scream broke through the night.

Rick jumped, slamming his head against the

too-low crushed ceiling. His pulse rocketing, he slipped from the Jeep. Though a mountain lion's scream supposedly sounded like a woman, he didn't think that was a mountain lion. He bolted toward Shay.

Through the brush, he saw the silhouette of a man with a submachine gun standing over her.

Instinct kicked in.

Knife in hand, Rick crept through the reeds and bushes with as much stealth as possible. Quietly, he closed the distance between the Jeep and their rudimentary camp. The guy was big, and Rick would get one shot at this.

Just one.

"Where is the other one?" The man jabbed the muzzle of his weapon at Shay.

Rick had the same question but in reference to a different man. Where was the other one of the killers? He scanned the perimeter.

"He's dead," she said.

The man jabbed her with his weapon. Rick couldn't stand there and let him kill her. Blinding rage exploded in Rick's veins. That, coupled with the element of surprise, would give him the chance he needed. He charged into the circle of firelight and knocked the automatic weapon from the man's grip. Before he could react, Rick drove him to the ground.

He pressed the blade of the buck knife to the man's throat. "Shay, grab the weapon."

The whites of the assailant's eyes shone with fear.

"Who are you? Why did you try to kill us?" Something about this man gnawed at his thoughts.

When the guy didn't speak, Rick pressed the knife against the flesh of his neck until it drew blood. "I'll ask you one more time. Who are you? Why are you after us?"

Then it hit him. This wasn't one of the two in the truck.

"Rick," Shay said, her voice tenuous, trembling.

He ignored her. She would try to talk him down.

"Rick!" This time, the blood-curdling demand in her tone let him know he'd better pay attention.

He hoped she was holding the weapon as he'd asked. Pressing the knife deeper into the man's throat—a simple, clear warning that he'd better not flinch—Rick turned his face halfway, keeping his focus split between the two of them.

Another man pointed a gun at her head.

SEVEN

The gun's muzzle bearing down on her temple, Shay fought to see straight, dizziness sweeping over her.

From the moment he'd turned his head, Rick had appeared frozen in time, standing over the man, the knife still pressing against the guy's throat. Rick locked eyes with her and the cold fear she saw in them nearly did her in.

He'd been a marine, for crying out loud. Didn't he have a plan? Was there anything he couldn't do? Blood roaring in her head, she practically screamed at him with her eyes to act.

Though his expression had turned to icy steel, she detected the answer in the slight movement of his head. Not yet. He wouldn't make his move yet, and wanted her to play along.

Her knees quivered, but she dared not allow them to buckle. One wrong move could be the end of them both. The metal dug painfully into her temple, though she refused to cower. But a small grunt under her breath gave her fear away.

Slowly, Rick removed the knife from the man's throat and spread his hands out, his non-threatening position letting them know he would submit. But he hadn't relinquished the knife when the man he'd threatened punched him in the gut. Rick's strong core apparently kept him from buckling as expected, so the guy went for Rick's face.

Rick sidestepped him and, with one split-second glance at Shay letting her know that now was the moment, he shoved his fist in the guy's face. Shay took her chance to make her own moves against her distracted attacker. She tried to kick him, but he was faster.

His arm wrapped around her throat.

Shay gasped for air.

The man fired a warning shot into the ground near where Rick struggled with the other one. A terror-filled screamed raced up her throat, but she caught and stifled it. Couldn't show her fear.

She might be pathetic and weak, but she wouldn't let them know. Shay had enough practice at acting tougher than she felt, but she'd never faced anything like this before.

"I'll say this just one time." The man's raspy voice, directed at Rick, buzzed against her ear. "If you cause any trouble, the woman dies."

Shay just wanted a chance to escape. A chance to live. At some point, this man would let his guard down and then she would have her chance. But that moment wasn't now.

Knocked on his back, Rick lay there, holding his hands up in surrender again—only this time, he meant it. Seeing him in that position crushed her insides, leaving her breathless. He'd tried, she'd give him that. But what could he do when she'd been used to bring about his compliance? Bitterness flooded her mouth.

If Shay hadn't been there, Rick might have gained his freedom quickly. He might have found his brother already.

Rick rose slowly to his feet while the other guy wiped his bloody nose on the sleeve of his camouflage down parka.

"What do you want with us?" Rick asked.

The man standing over Rick grabbed his automatic weapon. "You ask too many questions."

Questions. Was that why they'd been pursued? Because they'd asked about Aiden?

Shay wondered if that meant the men would kill her and Rick and make sure they were dead this time. Though she couldn't read Rick's hard expression, she didn't think he would go down without a fight. Neither would she. But wouldn't they already be dead if that was all these men had intended?

"First your buddies try to kill us by running us off the road," Rick said. "Then—"

"You hear that, Joey? Somebody tried to kill them."

"Shut your mouth."

"That means—"

"I said shut up. It means nothing."

"Kemp needs to—"

Joey stood in the man's face. "Shut. Your. Trap. We've got a job to do. So we do it. Let Kemp decide the rest."

Shay shared a glance with Rick. So this had to do with the man whose plane they had come to repossess after all. But where did the mining claim come into it?

"What job?" Rick asked.

"Shut up," both men yelled at Rick.

Somebody tried to kill them.... What was going on? Everything had happened so fast. Though she hadn't had long to see the men in the truck up close, she'd stared into the driver's eyes. Neither of the men possessed the same dark, sinister eyes of the driver who'd pushed them over.

The two sounded as if they were from Long Island or somewhere back East—not that same native Alaskan accent she'd heard from the truck's driver and passenger as the men discussed their demise only a few yards above them.

"Tie them up, then let's get moving," Joey said.

Joey's partner grunted. "My hands are frozen already. We've been at this all day."

"Then tie them up and stoke the fire. But we can't be here all night." The man's gaze searched the darkness around them. Was he wondering about the other men who'd hunted Rick and Shay?

If only Rick had found his gun. Maybe things would be different at this moment. There were too many "if onlys" to think about.

Joey's partner pulled plastic ties from his coat pocket and forced Rick to put his hands together. He drew in a breath and worked his jaw while the guy bound his wrists.

Then he moved behind Rick and kicked his knees, forcing him to the ground again. "Sit."

After Shay's wrists were bound, she dropped next to Rick by the fire and across from Joey, who examined the handgun he'd held to her head. Shay could hardly believe her eyes. Was that Rick's gun? The one he'd been looking for? She wanted desperately to know but knew better than to ask.

His partner threw some more fuel on the flames.

The fallen trunk at their backs, Rick shifted closer, his body a superficial protective barrier next to her. "Lean against me and get some rest," he murmured under his breath.

"You should listen to him," Joey said to her.

His words surprised her. If anything, she'd figured he might kick Rick and tell him to shut up. Why would their captors care if she got enough rest?

She was too tired to ponder it for long. She leaned her head against Rick's broad shoulder and took what comfort she could in his presence.

What had Rick's brother gotten them into?

Rick maintained his composure, calmed his breathing and thought about everything that had occurred. He could have ended this quickly if Shay hadn't accompanied him to fetch his brother and to fix the broken aircraft.

Having her here made him weak. These men knew that and used it to the fullest.

And his experience from the past made him weaker—he couldn't stand to be so helpless and impotent, unable to save someone.

That alone ripped at his confidence.

In an attempt to settle his mind, Rick tried to think of what vulnerabilities these men might have that he could exploit. Everyone had a weakness, including these two goons, who thought he and Shay would go willingly with them. If he could figure out what they were after, he might be able to use it as a bargaining chip. But why would they bother with them? Why hadn't they simply killed them? The answer had to be they needed them alive for some reason that only Kemp knew about—but Rick wouldn't push that point.

How did all of this connect with Aiden and the plane? Clearly they hadn't known all there was to know about Buster Kemp.

He studied the two men who sat across the fire loosely guarding their captives. So confident they were that Rick and Shay wouldn't escape or even attempt to try that they paid them a bare minimum of attention.

The one called Joey examined the nine-millimeter and the grip glove that Rick had installed. Where had the guy found it? And why had he taken it? Clearly he had no need of it, because he and his partner carried their own lethal weapons. Unfortunately, the sight of the submachine guns brought back unwanted images. Rick couldn't bear to hear those weapons go off.

Shay had hated seeing his gun. He hated seeing theirs.

It was just another reason why Rick had no intention of hiking anywhere with these two. Why go deeper into the wilderness, farther away from a likely rescue and into the outlaws' camp?

He could think of only one justification—

Aiden. If there was a chance he was still alive, he had to be at the camp with those men. And if he was, then saving Shay *and* Aiden would become his task.

To do that, he'd have to be at the top of his game. Somehow Rick had to shove aside the doubts from the past that plagued him. Somehow he had to turn this around and get his advantage back. Rick squeezed his eyes closed, shutting out the firelight.

Those two idiots across the fire from him appeared too relaxed. Either that, or they were exhausted and they made the mistake of not hiding it well.

He could kick the flames into their eyes and Shay could make a run for it while he distracted them. And then what?

Face the Alaska bush on her own? He doubted she'd make it far before bullets riddled her back. Rick ground his molars.

He'd have to bide his time.

Finally, the gray light of an early Alaskan dawn colored the strip of sky visible from the gorge.

Joey sprung to his feet and started kicking dirt on the fire. "Time to go."

Rick didn't much feel like cooperating, but he had to think of Shay and Aiden. Wrists bound, Rick maneuvered to his knees, then stood.

Shay shrank away when Joey tried to assist her to her feet. Rick seethed at the man for touching her, but he hid his distaste lest it cause Shay more harm. The guy might like to mess with her just to get at Rick.

Men could be animals. Rick had seen that for himself too many times.

Joey got in Rick's face and smirked. "Pretty impressive that you survived that fall."

How did the guy know so much if he wasn't involved in the crash?

"Yeah, I know about that. It was my job to make sure you made it to the camp. But then I couldn't find you anywhere. Except I saw the fire from the road." Joey held up a night-vision scope hanging from the strap on his weapon. "Saw the Jeep at the bottom of the gorge. Saw her. She was in the picture. So I knew you're the ones."

Rick's heart hammered. Two men tried to prevent them from making the mining camp, and these men were abducting them to take them there. *Aiden, what have you done?*

"What do you know about the men who tried to kill us? What is going on?" Rick steadied his voice. "What do you want with us?"

"I said too much as it is. My point is that I don't know how you survived, but I won't underestimate you. Since I know you're resourceful, I'm going to give it to you straight. We have a ways to go. If you try anything, she gets hurt in a thousand ways you can't even imagine."

Rick wanted to wring his neck. He inched forward— *Hold it together.*

Joey smirked again, satisfied that he'd achieved his goal of getting a rise out of Rick. "And as an added bonus, if you try anything, you won't see your brother."

Rick's pulse spiked at those last words.

"Aiden…" His breaths came too fast. "Where's my brother? Why are you holding him?"

Though he'd hoped against hope that Aiden was somewhere safe, his suspicions were now confirmed—these men had his brother. Hearing the man refer to his brother had been too much.

Joey pressed the tip of Rick's own gun into his chest. If Rick weren't bound, he'd quickly disarm the guy—didn't he know that? But it wasn't the gun that held Rick in place. It was Joey's leer and the threats he'd made that still rang in Rick's ears. "You'll find out soon enough. Just remember what I said. One wrong move on your part and you get to watch people you care about suffer because of you."

Rick felt as if he were in the Middle East again, staked out in the desert. Shay was the stake used on one side and Aiden the one on the other.

Joey's partner strapped the automatic weapon across his broad chest and hiked from their crude camp. Joey motioned for Rick to follow and then Shay. Joey would pull up the rear, ready to harm Shay using Rick's gun if necessary.

Surreal.

Before Rick did as he was told, he moved close to Shay and whispered, "Don't worry. It's going to be okay."

He hoped she read in his eyes the words he couldn't say. How sorry he was about this, and that he had every intention of making a grand escape. That he needed her to hold it together, to play along for as long as needed. All things he couldn't say out loud.

To say that terror emanated from her wide eyes was an understatement, and yet she stood tall, held her head high. He was glad that Shay was a strong person, but as a woman she couldn't blend in and pretend she was one of the guys when they got to the camp. Would she be strong enough to face the challenges ahead? His need to protect her stirred to a new level.

In response to his optimistic words—unusual for him—she gave a subtle nod. She was with him.

He could only hope their shared resolve would be enough to get through whatever they were about to face.

EIGHT

Riding in the utility ATV on steroids, Shay wasn't sure how much more of the rough trail she could take, especially with her wrists bound so she couldn't hang on to anything. Rick was even less fortunate—his ankles had also been tied together and the men had hefted him into the cargo bed like a bag of Idaho potatoes. It had been painful to watch. Rick was a strong man with military training. That he'd been reduced to this...

Shay sighed. They'd trekked through the gorge until she'd thought she couldn't take another step, and then come upon the ATVs and the trail. She wanted to protest or try to find a way to escape, but she fought the urge. Breaking free of the situation wasn't survivable unless something changed in their favor. Rick knew that. She knew that.

In the meantime, she'd watch and wait for his move.

Don't wait too long, Rick.

Of course, he wanted and needed to get to that camp to find his brother. That had been their goal all along, but not as captives. That wouldn't help Aiden.

Eventually the trees surrounding their path broke away and the terrain completely changed into a full-blown settlement of buildings and tractors surrounding a hole in the ground and a pile of dirt. Not a rock quarry, exactly. Something less elegant. A gravel pit. This small section of pristine, beautiful Alaska had morphed into an ugly mining camp.

Shay drew in a breath as realization struck— it *was* a pit, only of a different kind than the gravel ones she'd seen before. This was a gold-mining pit.

The plane had to be around there somewhere and that meant the airstrip was nearby, too. Shay sat up, taking it all in. She glanced at her captor, who whipped the ATV in and out, making his way through grooves in dried mud to the buildings.

This didn't seem like an ordinary gold-mining camp. There were a dozen or so men, and more than half of them brandished automatic weapons. Was that normal? Was there so much gold pouring from that hole that these men felt they needed to protect it?

A sick feeling roiled in her stomach. *What was going on here?*

Unfortunately, the ATV didn't go unnoticed, and Shay received more than a few looks before they finally pulled up in front of a small wood-framed building with a tin roof. It was just one of several buildings at the camp.

Joey climbed from the ATV and pointed his weapon at Shay. "Get out."

She didn't need to be told twice, and by the time she made it to the ground, Rick was out of the cargo bed and stood next to her. At least they'd untied his ankles.

"Sit down next to the Wolverine." He meant the ATV, Shay assumed.

On the cold ground? Why didn't they just leave her and Rick in the vehicle?

Joey left them at his partner's mercy and tromped away. He entered the building without so much as a glance behind him.

His partner nudged the end of his weapon under Shay's chin and leaned in, an unpleasant grin on his face.

"Do as he says, Shay." Rick's tone left no room for argument, but she hated hearing the defeat in it.

Against the Wolverine, Rick slid to the ground and Shay followed. Cold quickly seeped into her legs. A backhoe rumbled from across the camp, digging into the earth, and a generator hummed. Diesel exhaust poisoned what should have been some of the cleanest air on Earth.

Once their guard distanced himself from them, Shay leaned closer to Rick.

"What are they going to do with us? What should we do?"

Rick stared ahead, his features as hard as granite. "As soon as I find my brother, we're leaving." Then, as he turned to face her, his expression softened. "Or maybe sooner. I need to get you out of here. When I think it's safe for you, I'll make my move."

What if it was never safe for her? And how could he make a move when they were both held captive? "You act like we're here by choice. That when you decide we're leaving, we can just walk out of here."

Rick sagged against the tire and stared straight ahead. Was he just giving up? He could at least try to convince her otherwise. Shay hadn't meant to sound that harsh, but she was exhausted. Frustrated. Caked in the grime of the outdoors.

She swung her gaze back to him. Dust covered his face and neck and the man still looked good. "I trust you to get us out of here. Just tell me what to do, and I'll do it."

His grin was tenuous, but it still lifted her spirits. "I'm glad to hear you say that."

"Can you give me a hint of what to expect?"

"I hate to say I haven't worked it out yet. But stay alert. Keep strong."

"Great."

"I've always admired that about you."

"Admired what?"

"Your strength. On the inside and out."

"A lot of good that does me here."

"You'll make some man a good wife one day."

Some man. Just not him. Where had that thought come from? "My dad used to say that." Daddy had hoped she'd find someone and get married before he finally died of the disease that had eaten away at him. They'd had to sell his business just to keep up with the medical bills. She knew he'd wanted her to have someone to lean on, to help her through losing him and getting her life back on track. But in the end, she'd been able to do it on her own. Her dad had raised her to take care of herself, and she had planned to keep it that way. "You know, I'm not horse flesh to be traded or sold to the highest bidder."

"Shay," he said, his voice more gentle than she'd ever heard it. "That wasn't meant to be an insult."

"I know." Tears burned behind her eyes, but she blinked them into submission. Why the sudden jab of emotion? This situation was breaking her down, and fast.

Shouting ensued from inside the building. Joey's partner, who'd been pacing the rudimentary decking and smoking a cigarette, froze. He flicked the butt into a puddle and glanced at them, a worried look on his face, confirming that Shay and Rick must be the topic of the argument.

Three consecutive gunshots fired off inside.

Shay's heart jackknifed. They hadn't seen the worst of this yet.

Wrists still bound, Rick shifted to his knees and then got to his feet, setting the guard on edge. From the deck, he rolled his shoulders as if he was about to show his displeasure, except he hesitated, appearing indecisive. He paced in front of the door, weighing his options. Rick couldn't understand why he hadn't barged straight into the structure to see what had happened. Was it really so common around here for guards to fire their weapons off when they got angry?

That could make things tougher for Rick and Shay. But then again, a group of cutthroats who couldn't agree on things meant that he and Shay might actually have a chance to break away. Men who were divided like this were easily distracted—and if he'd noticed anything about these men, it was that they were preoccupied. He might even say troubled.

And definitely not united. After listening to Joey and his partner, Rick didn't get the sense that they were loyal to anyone, and that meant a power struggle was probably already in progress. No one knew who was really in charge because it could change at any moment.

The situation was definitely unstable. The fact that two other guys had tried to kill them just added more explosives to the package. And that meant they had to find a way to escape as soon as possible. Hopefully lack of strong leadership would give them an opportunity to exploit that weakness before the situation got truly ugly. The last thing he wanted was for him, Shay and Aiden to end up in the middle of a cross fire, especially since he'd seen that this group of men was carrying as much firepower as a law enforcement entity, the military or organized crime. He frowned at the thought.

Shay climbed to her feet and stood a little behind him. He liked that she wasn't the type of person who easily caved under pressure, but he also liked that she was willing to let him protect her. He *wanted* to protect her. In fact, that innate desire seemed to be expanding inside him where she was concerned. Problem was, he'd prefer she wasn't even here at all.

He hoped she'd taken note of the firepower, too, so she'd understand they'd stepped into an extremely volatile situation.

Just when the guard looked as if he would march down the timber steps and tell them to drop to the ground again, the door behind him swung open. He whirled around to confront Joey, whose face was that of an angry bear.

Joey glared at Shay and Rick and motioned them over. Rick wanted to stand his ground, make him work for it rather than just obey their every command, but the three gunshots were fresh in his mind.

Rick trudged forward, Shay on his heels, their warnings about hurting her, hurting his brother, clinging to his thoughts. Dread rolled over him like a glacier, cold and heavy.

He and Shay were about to face off with the man in charge today. The source of all their troubles.

He sucked in a breath and calmed his thoughts. He couldn't overreact or lose it. He had to play this right for Shay's sake. For his brother's sake. But more so for Shay—she was the lone woman, as far as he could tell, in this camp of cutthroat gold miners.

Rick reached the covered decking, making sure that Shay was right behind him. Joey eyed her, and Rick ground his molars, holding him self in check. He wanted to give the guy what he deserved, but too many muscles with guns surrounded them.

Bracing himself, Rick stepped through the door into a smoke-filled room where two additional men waited. One sat on the other side of a messy desk. Rick assumed this was Kemp. A stocky man with fierce eyes, he wore a lumberjack shirt and looked to be in his late forties. He kept his hand pressed over the grip of a gun resting in front of him on the desk.

Rick's gun.

His lips slipped into an angry frown when he looked at Rick. Then when Shay stepped in behind him, Kemp covered his mouth and rubbed his chin in thought, as if he didn't know what to do with them. But that had to be wrong. Joey and his partner had been sent specifically to find them, hadn't they?

"Give me a few minutes." He glared at the others.

A few seconds later Rick and Shay were alone in the office with him.

"Go ahead, have a seat," he said.

Rick preferred to stand and give the illusion that he had more power.

The man got up and turned his back to them. "Coffee?"

Neither of them answered.

Patience running thin, Rick stepped closer to the desk. "What is going on here? Why did somebody try to kill us? Why have we been abducted?"

The man nodded, letting Rick know that he'd heard the questions. Scowling, Kemp poured his coffee and sat back down. "The attempt on your life was an unfortunate event that I had nothing to do with. If it were left to me, you would have found your way here on your own in search of the plane and your brother. When you didn't show, I sent my men to look for you. They knew you'd been in town and that something was wrong. That's when they spotted the fire and decided to investigate. But they didn't try to kill you."

"But they took us captive. Brought us here at gunpoint. They threatened to kill us if we resisted. Here we sit in your office with our wrists still bound. And if they didn't try to kill us, then who did?"

Rick decided to take that seat after all, and Shay sat next to him. Exhaustion played across her features.

"You're here because of your brother. And as to the men who tried to kill you, you survived." Dread flashed in his eyes before angry resolve rose in its place. "I can't tell you more than that."

Rick didn't see it the same way but knew he

wouldn't get more out of Kemp on that point. He edged forward in the seat. "Let me see him."

"That's not going to happen. Not until I have your full cooperation."

"Cooperation?"

He took a sip of his coffee, watching Rick over the rim of his cup. Measuring him. "Those men who found and brought you to the camp answer to me only to a point. You see, Mr. Savage— That is your name, isn't it?"

Rick frowned in reply. He didn't like the man knowing so much about him, especially when he knew close to nothing about Kemp. "And you must be Buster Kemp." The restaurant owner from Chicago and obviously much more.

The man nodded. "What else do you know about me besides my name?"

"Nothing. We came for the plane. We don't need to know anything else. I'd rather just take my brother and get out of here, forget we were ever here."

"It's too late for that. There's something I need from you, and if I have to use your brother as leverage to get it, then so be it. I've got too much at stake here to accept no for an answer. You see, you and I are in the same situation. We're both prisoners."

Rick glanced at Shay, trying to read what she thought. Her frown said it all.

"I owe serious money to the wrong man," Kemp continued. "I was desperate and had to use my grandfather's mining claim as leverage. Instead of killing me, he sent me here with his men to work the claim. I have this one mining season to dig up enough gold to repay him. *With* interest. So far we've found next to nothing. If we don't strike something big soon, I'm as good as dead."

"You can't just mine a claim and expect success unless you know what you're doing."

"My grandfather taught me all I need to know. Believe me. If there's gold here, we'll find it. And if we don't find anything…I have a backup plan." He scooted forward and leaned closer. "I'm the lone pilot in this group of clowns. And my plane is the only one here. If I use it to leave in a hurry, they won't be able to come after me, and by the time they use alternate means to track me down, I'll already be long gone."

So the plane was the man's escape hatch if things didn't go right. "That's why you took Aiden—you couldn't let him leave with your only means of escape."

Kemp nodded. "It was just bad timing on his part. I figured I'd delay him a few days before leaving. But then we started finding flecks of gold. We're this close—" he held his forefinger near his thumb "—to striking it rich."

Rick leaned against the chair back. The man's face was flushed, sweat beading his brow. "You have gold fever. You're blinded by it now. So you figure you'll just delay us along with Aiden?"

Kemp clasped his hands behind his head and leaned back in his chair, smiling. "I remember when my grandfather got gold fever—it was infectious, contagious. People don't usually find big nuggets in Alaska. Anything over a few ounces isn't common. But then he found a nugget weighing in at thirty troy ounces. Before he died and left the claim to me, my grandfather took all the money from the gold and invested in the camp and the heavy equipment needed to dig out the rest. I made the mistake of opening my mouth, but I had no choice. In the end, I'm glad I had the claim to use as leverage."

"I don't get it. Why do you owe someone money when you have a whole gold claim?" Rick asked.

A contemplative look came across Kemp's face, then he finally answered. "Gold mining is always going to have its risks. Long hours of hard, manual labor with no guarantees. My father didn't share my grandfather's obsession and started a restaurant business before I was born. I grew up learning that business and made it my own. I spent a few summers with my grandfather, but I'd nearly forgotten about this place.

At least when I needed it, it was still here and waiting for me."

Rick studied the man. He was a salesman; no doubt there. Had sold the guy he owed with the idea that he'd be able to mine enough gold to pay him back. Rick didn't know how much he owed, but he could guess it had to be a large sum.

"The men have already seen the gold for themselves." Kemp grinned. "All of them have gold fever now."

Kemp had counted on that reaction.

"And no one is going to stand in their way," Rick said.

"Now you understand. By the time I found out your brother was expecting you, the damage was done. I couldn't let him go. I don't need anyone sniffing around, asking questions or causing trouble. The problem is the men here don't exactly answer to me. They answer to the guy I owe. They didn't kill you, because, well, I convinced them it wouldn't be in their best interest. Don't make me change my mind on that."

"Just how long do you think you can keep us here before someone comes in search of us?"

Kemp shrugged. "Let them come. You're not here. We never saw you."

Rick believed the guy had it in him to persuade these men to do whatever he wanted, but he still wasn't sure why he'd kept them alive.

They knew too much and could use that against him. "You mentioned needing something from us. What is it?"

"Work the claim with us and in a few days, when I've paid back what I owe, you can see your brother and all of you leave here richer. Just take me with you."

Yeah, right. Rick didn't believe Kemp's story. They were as good as dead any way you looked at it. What reason would he have to let them live when they could cause so much trouble for him? The way the guy looked at Shay...

The airplane.

He needed a mechanic to fix it so he could fly it out. Idiot. If he weren't close to exhaustion, he would have realized that before. Kemp needed Shay for that—that was why they were here. Aiden had told these men far too much, putting Shay's life at stake. Kemp wanted to work the claim, find the gold and then make his great escape. Rick doubted he even intended to pay back the man he owed.

And once the plane was repaired, he'd leave Rick and Shay behind to face certain death at the hands of these cutthroats.

"Do we have a deal?" the snake asked.

Rick had forgotten he'd been offered one and hesitated.

"Doesn't sound like you've given us much

choice," Shay said, speaking up for the first time since entering the office.

"You have a choice. It's either work with me or die."

"Let me get this straight," Rick said. "You've abducted us and conscripted us into slaving away at your gold mine, and any attempts at escape are on pain of death."

The guy leaned forward, a sinister grin across his face. "Yes."

NINE

"The point is, you're not free to leave. Act like you're worth something around here, and I can convince the others to leave you alone."

Shay watched the exchange between Rick and Kemp. How long did the guy plan to hold them? And how did he plan to do it? If they were made to work, he couldn't keep them tied up the whole time. How long would it take before Connor became concerned, and if he even found them, would that be too late? Like Kemp already said, he might come looking, but none of the henchmen would admit they were here.

Uncertainty bombarded her.

Shay lifted her wrists to get Kemp's attention. "We can't work like this."

He moved around to the front of the desk and sat on the edge. "Now that's more like it. You see my dilemma, don't you? My hands are tied, too—I can't let you leave until we've struck gold and settled my debts."

"And then what?" Shay almost wished she hadn't asked, but it was better knowing the answer than going crazy wondering. "You'll just let us go?"

"Something like that—if you behave and don't make any trouble." He scratched his head, appearing to consider his next words. "I'll need that plane fixed, too, without letting them know my plans. If they find out, then all bets are off. Your lives, my life—they're all forfeit."

"I'll need my tools. They were in the Jeep."

"There are plenty of tools here for fixing the equipment. Depending on what went wrong, if you can't make them work, we'll go back to the Jeep to get your things."

"Not just the tools. The Jeep also had the part I brought to fix what we think is wrong."

Kemp eyed her as though trying to read the truth. "I'll send Joey to bring back what he can find in the Jeep. Hopefully that'll include what you need without me having to be specific."

"You think they don't already know what you're planning?" Rick ground out the words.

"They suspect, which is why they walk around with the guns. They still have to follow most of my orders since I'm the only one who knows how to extract the gold. But I'm under guard, too, which makes it all a little awkward, being in charge and under guard."

He removed the plastic ties around Shay's wrists but left Rick's on. His gaze pierced Shay's. "Try anything and your friend here gets hurt. He'll suffer before he dies. Any wrong moves from either of you and you'll be locked away like the other one. You won't see each other again. Am I clear? There's no law here to keep them in line. There's only me and their boss. Don't give them a reason to hurt you."

Shay frowned. The man knew how to use leverage effectively. Shay watched Rick's jaw working, the pulse at his temple beating as he exerted effort to hold in his displeasure. She eyed Kemp. If Rick could pin him down, she could probably get the weapon. But they couldn't simply walk out of the building with the gun-toting men standing on the porch and all around the camp. Kemp had made that all too clear. From what she'd overheard from Joey and his cohort on the trip to the mine, she got the feeling that the men were getting bored just waiting for an excuse to blow someone away.

Gunfire in rapid succession drove home that thought. Kemp grabbed the gun off the desk—splintering Shay's idea to grab it herself—and bolted for the door, forgetting about his accidental prisoners.

"What's going on?" he yelled at the guards he'd turned into unlikely miners.

He stepped through and the door closed behind him, leaving Shay and Rick alone. "Hurry, untie me," Rick said.

Shay whipped around the desk and opened the drawer to find something to cut Rick free. Kemp had taken the knife he'd used to cut her ties off.

"Never mind—I hear someone coming. Get over here. Shay. Now."

She glanced up to see the alarm in his eyes, along with overwhelming concern for her. "If I can just grab something to free—"

The door swung open and in walked Kemp. When he saw where she stood, his face took on a whole new look that made Shay wish she'd done as Rick had asked. He glared at Shay. She stood frozen, her hand on his open desk drawer. She couldn't move under his visual assault.

"See, now, this is what I'm talking about. I thought we had an agreement." He stomped around the desk and yanked her arm away from the drawer.

She let it go with a yelp.

"Leave her alone." Rick's voice was a low growl. "I asked her to untie me. Thought you'd forgotten about me, that's all."

Shay got the sense that he was ready to pounce over the top of the desk and take the man down, even with his wrists still bound, if Kemp tried to hurt her.

Kemp must have sensed it, too, because he released her. "I'll untie you as soon as I march you out to see what I meant when I said tensions are running high. Either of you got any medical experience? Know how to stop a man from bleeding to death?"

At the mention of blood, Shay felt hers drain from her face. She watched Rick's features pale as well, and not because he hadn't seen enough blood in his life. Probably because he didn't like to see those he wanted to protect—her and Aiden—caught in the middle of this.

Kemp waved Rick's gun at them. "Let's go."

Someone had been shot. Rick probably knew what to do, considering his military training. But would he help these people?

Shay trudged around the desk and opened the door for Rick. When he passed her, all she could think was that if he were alone, and she wasn't here to stand in his way or rein him in, he'd probably have made his way free already and found Aiden. He'd be willing to risk getting shot. But as it stood, he was biding his time, waiting for the right opportunity to get them out before this whole situation turned on them. Shay didn't believe the desperate, crazy man who wasn't really in charge. She doubted Rick believed the man, either. He wouldn't simply let them walk away.

The fact was obvious considering his *own* plans didn't include walking away. No. He planned to fly out of this and leave them all behind. Kemp kept the firearm at his side pointed at the earth as he walked next to them, and the other two, Joey and his partner, accompanied them as they followed Kemp through the mining camp.

She counted five buildings in all. A main house, which might or might not have a kitchen and bedrooms. What looked like a bunkhouse, a storage building and two more buildings, one that could pass for a cabin with living quarters. That was her best guess without seeing inside.

Not a large operation, but not a recreational mining camp either, as far as she could tell. She knew little about modern-day gold mining. But one thing she did know, these men meant to dig up gold. What she couldn't figure was why. If what Kemp said was true and he owed someone money, the camp itself was worth a small fortune if you counted the equipment. Add to that the gold that had already been found and the potential of more to come. Why not sell it?

Maybe he'd already tried.

As they approached the building next to the bunkhouse, a man's screams and moans could be heard. The sound wrapped around her guts and squeezed. Soon enough, two men appeared from behind the building dragging another injured man, blood oozing from a gunshot wound in his leg.

"What happened?" Rick asked.

"A couple of the men have been at odds since we arrived. I guess they were playing Russian roulette or chicken. I don't know." Kemp's voice was strained. "All I know is that we're short-handed on men already and can't spare this one, even if he is an idiot to play around with loaded guns. We need to get at the gold before the weather turns bad in more ways than one."

He eyed Rick. "Your brother told me you both served in the U.S. Marines. Can you help? Know what to do here?"

Rick flinched. "He needs a doctor."

"He won't get one in time. Not out here. You gonna watch him die?"

"Are you telling me you've got all this fire-power around and you don't have anyone who knows how to treat wounds? Not to mention other potential accidents?"

"Not anymore." Kemp's eyes went brutal.

What did that mean? Had someone escaped or been killed?

"And no one else who might have a clue about what they're doing is willing to step up to the plate," Kemp added. "Stand out in the crowd."

Shaking his head, Rick held up his wrists. "Not much I can do like this."

"You have a point." Kemp pulled out the knife and cut the ties.

"I need your medical kit. Survival kit. Something. Tell me you at least have one of those."

"Of course we do." Kemp yelled at one of his guards to take the injured man inside and find the kit.

Shay followed Kemp and Rick inside, where they shoved a couple of tables together and laid the man on the hard surface. The room was messy with boxes and supplies and smelled like tobacco smoke and booze. Like a place where the men hung out to play cards.

The injured man continued to moan, his face losing color. Blood was quickly spreading along the table and onto the floor. Shay shrank into a dark corner—this was out of her league, not to mention that the sight of the blood made her weak and dizzy. She could serve Rick better by staying out of the way and out of trouble.

While waiting on the medical kit, Rick tied off the guy's leg with a tourniquet, then ripped his pants to expose the wound. A man who looked a little too young to be in with this brutal group held the briefcase-size kit out to Rick. He searched through until he found what he needed.

Shay couldn't stand to look, so she shut her

eyes. That only seemed to magnify the man's grunts of pain and curses as Rick worked. She wished Kemp would let her leave. But this was meant to be seared into her thoughts so she'd remember what could happen to her should she try to leave.

What if the man didn't survive? Would Rick pay the price?

With that, Shay realized her own predicament—what if she couldn't fix the plane? What if there was more wrong than could be fixed with a simple part replacement?

Any direction her thoughts turned only led her to every death-defying risk they faced. Shay forced her eyes open and watched Rick press gauze over the wound and tape it in place.

"The Combat Gauze will control the bleeding," he said, "until you can get him to a doctor, which I am *not*. He needs an IV with fluids. Could need a blood transfusion, too."

Kemp argued with the other men in the room about what to do with the injured man and the one who shot him. Rick eased back and away from the quarrel. His gaze slid to Shay. At that moment she knew he'd never lost track of her— even with all the chaos, he'd somehow always known where she was. That awareness sent warmth through her and an insane sense of security. She could almost imagine that he'd always been in control. That he was in control even now.

But she wouldn't lie to herself.

Still, the way he'd handled treating the wounded man under the pressure spiked her admiration. The urge to run to him, hoping he'd wrap her in his arms, engulfed her. But she didn't want to feel the pain that came with counting on someone. Trusting someone. She couldn't let herself feel this way about anyone—especially him.

Remember...remember when he almost killed you, his finger against the trigger guard before he realized what he was doing.

Shay stepped back, deeper into the corner.

Hurt skated across his dark gunmetal grays.

Funny how the small, subtle step back she'd taken pierced like shrapnel. What was that about? Why'd she do it? Why'd he care? She made him think she didn't look at him any differently than she viewed the rest of them here, the herd of thugs in the room.

What are you doing, man?

He couldn't let her get to him like that. Not if he wanted to protect her. Get her to safety. He needed to keep his thoughts on target.

The shouting grew louder. If this turned nasty, he needed a way out, and fast.

Rick clenched his fists, squeezing them until they hurt. While these men were distracted by the injured one—a man Rick figured would die sooner rather than later if they didn't get him more intensive medical attention—he could catch them off guard. Take one of their weapons…but he knew all too well the fight that would then ensue.

The guarantee of more to be injured, including Shay.

Even if they made it out alive, where was his brother being kept? He needed to rescue him, too.

Clench fist. Relax. Clench. Relax.

Shay suddenly started toward him, gliding across the room in stealth mode. His hopes that no one would notice her were quickly dashed. The shouting fell silent. Kemp, startled by Shay moving to Rick's side, acted as if he finally remembered he had guests. Or prisoners.

"Deal with it," he said to the others, gesturing to the wounded man, who had fallen unconscious.

Rick sent up a silent prayer for the man. He had been trained to deal with this and had done the best he could with what he'd been given. That and prayer were all he had to give.

When Shay bumped up against Rick, he wanted to slip his arm around her waist and tug her close to reassure her. Or maybe, if he was honest, to reassure himself.

But not with Kemp watching.

The man left the others to take care of their wounded and focused on Rick and Shay. But before he could speak, Shay took a step toward him. "We haven't eaten anything since yesterday. If we're going to stay and work, can we get some sleep and something to eat?"

Really? Rick should have thought of that, but he didn't much feel like negotiating with this man or even suggesting that he had any intention of agreeing to his deal. On the other hand, Kemp would more likely acquiesce to Shay's request, coming from her, even though Rick had demonstrated he was willing to cooperate by showing these men how to use their simple medical kit. Or had that been simply a test? More than likely it had been.

Confirming Rick's thought, Kemp cut a sliver-eyed gaze Rick's way. "Let's go."

Before he made a move, though, he headed for the table and grabbed the abandoned submachine gun. He glanced at the other men to see who it belonged to, then scowled and took the weapon for his own, slinging it across his shoulder. He thrust Rick's gun into his pocket, then turned his attention on Rick.

Rick got the message loud and clear. *Mess with me and I'll kill you myself.*

Rick finally decided how to read Kemp. He had put on a subtle but warm and friendly demeanor in his office, making sure to season that with warnings about the other men—the men he'd promised to keep in check if Rick and Shay would do their parts—but it was all for show. He was really a brute himself, just like the rest of these guys, or else he couldn't hope to have any measure of control over them. With their accents and mannerisms, they reminded Rick of mobsters. He wondered if he'd eventually hear mention of a familiar crime-family name. Gambini, Stefazzi, Feroli?

"You coming?"

A cool blast of air accompanied Kemp's voice and yanked Rick from his thoughts. Kemp stood in the jamb of the opened door, staring at Rick. Waiting on Shay, who hadn't left his side.

Rick and Shay followed him through the door, leaving behind the unconscious gunshot victim. Guilt threaded his thoughts. He'd already assessed the situation. He'd prayed. Other than that, it was out of his hands.

As they stepped outside again, Rick noted that the temperature had warmed up a little with the sun. Depending on what sort of labor he was made to do, he might even work up a sweat. He

could probably go without a coat for a few hours.
But he wondered how long it would last. If they
made an escape, they needed the weather to cooperate. Interior Alaska wasn't the place to get
caught unprepared, and they were already in the
middle of autumn. Could probably expect a few
prewinter warning storms. If they were going to
get away, their timing would have to be perfect.
And they *had* to get away as soon as possible.

They were caught in the middle of a battle between the ranks over an unproved gold claim.
Was there really enough gold here to satisfy
these greedy, murderous men? Rick considered
what it might feel like to discover gold in whatever form—dust or nuggets. Unbidden, a chill
of anticipation ran through him.

Hinting at much cooler weather to come, a
gusty breeze slapped across Rick's face, startling him. Realization gripped his insides. What
was he thinking? He wasn't here for the gold.
He shook off the craziness. He couldn't possibly
succumb to the frenzy of finding gold.

The group approached another building and
Kemp shoved through the door, followed by
Shay and Rick and a weapon-toting guard dog.
If they had to live like this—followed around
by men carrying deadly weapons—it wouldn't
be much of an existence. But he had no intention of staying that long.

Kemp escorted them into another building. 'This is our mess hall, as we call it. But the cook's out for the moment." Kemp's eyes crinkled around the corners when he looked at Shay.

Rick's gut burned at the reference to this place as the mess hall—a term usually used to denote the meal space used by military men, police officers or firemen. Heroes.

These men at the mining camp were anything but that. Nor did Rick like the warm fuzzy looks that Kemp had given Shay so far, though she pretended not to notice.

"Have a seat and I'll see what I can find for you to eat. I don't want to cook anything I don't have to. We need to conserve our energy." Kemp opened the pantry and stared inside.

Rick's guard dog stood near the door and didn't take his eyes off Rick. Shay slipped out of her coat and sat in a folding chair at the long table. Kemp's grandfather had a decent setup here, or had Kemp brought all this in for these men? But while everything seemed well situated, Rick's doubt grew that Kemp would be able to deliver on his repayment plan, considering the cost to run this operation—it would take a whole lot of gold to see any sort of profit.

Especially at a few ounces at a time.

"How about a can of chili? Quicker than frozen burritos."

"Sounds good," Shay said.

Sitting across from Rick, she slid her hand over the table, then stopped just before reaching his. Rick found himself wishing she'd gone the whole distance. Though he wasn't sure why, since he couldn't find it in himself to meet her halfway.

"Is he going to be all right? The man who got shot?" Though she whispered the question it was easily heard in the quiet room, only big enough to seat twenty or so people comfortably at the long tables.

Rick shook his head and frowned. He'd done all he could, but the man needed the kind of medical attention he could get from a doctor with more equipment at hand. Rick held on to hope they would send the wounded man to a hospital but knew that that would raise questions. Unfortunately, that was the exact reason they probably wouldn't get the man help.

Kemp served bowls of chili and glasses of water. Oddly enough, he remained at the other end of the table looking over papers that someone had brought in to him. Next to him rested a case containing a satellite phone. His posture spoke of a man who had work to do and couldn't waste any more time on them. If Rick had his way, Kemp would simply forget about them. By biding their time, avoiding attention and persuading Kemp and his men they were anxious to see gold, too, they might gain their greatest chance of escape. Rick would have time to learn where his brother was being kept, as well. He hoped.

A myriad of thoughts and emotions coursing through him, he and Shay finished up the meal in silence. From the other end of the table, Kemp suddenly stood, his chair scraping the floor.

"I haven't figured out where to put you in the workflow yet." He looked at the guard and nodded.

The man standing like a sentinel at the door moved toward Rick. "Come with me."

Reluctantly, Rick stood. "Where are we going?"

"He's taking you to your quarters, where you can wait until called upon. Get some rest while you're there. Don't forget you need to prove that you're an asset worth keeping alive to more than just me."

Shay stood, too.

"No, you stay with me," Kemp said.

TEN

Her gaze locked with Rick's. When her mouth dropped open in silent protest, Rick filled in "No, she doesn't."

Heart pounding in her ears, she scraped her chair across the floor as she rushed to Rick's side. "Please, we need to stay together."

Kemp gathered the papers on the table before he answered. "Don't worry. You'll be safer with me than with him. Plus, I don't need you two making big escape plans together."

Rick grabbed Shay's hand and stepped in front of her to face off with Kemp as he approached them. "Look, I don't intend to leave without my brother. Per your proposal, if we help you, then we get to leave *with* Aiden when all of this is over. Why would I make any plans that would put that at risk? And if it's all the same to you, I'll be the one who's protecting her."

The way he said those words, and his protective stance, almost made Shay's fear melt away

Big strong Rick, standing up for her. She could almost believe he felt *something* for her. But she was afraid for him, too. What would Kemp do to him for facing off with him like this?

"I don't have time to argue. If you're going to be a problem, I'll just lock you away from the light of day until this is over. But you can't protect her without a weapon, and you're not getting your hands on one."

The fact that the bad guy was discussing with Rick how best to protect the lone woman in a mining camp full of criminals dawned on Shay. Her breaths started coming too fast.

Calm. Down.

Inhale.

Exhale.

"I could dispose of them for you," the silent sentinel said, throwing in his opinion.

"That's something to consider if I can't get cooperation around here." Kemp scowled at the guard when he passed Rick and Shay and headed to the exit. "We're running out of time, Savage. Gold-mining season is coming to a close. The weather is going to turn. Get some rest and we'll put you to work later today or tomorrow."

Shay sucked in a breath to calm her haywire pulse. She could do this. For Rick. For them. Maybe everything would be all right. Maybe she would be safer with Kemp than with Rick, considering he was the man in charge. Sort of.

When she stepped from behind Rick to show Kemp she'd agree, Rick pressed her behind him again, squeezing her hand. His was strong and warm, and she wished she could keep hold of it, but she tugged herself free and pushed past him.

"It's okay, Rick." She moved to Kemp and turned around to look at Rick. She hated what she saw in his eyes—he thought that she didn't believe he could protect her. That she didn't trust him. Believe in him. It was the same look she'd seen earlier today after he'd treated the wounded man. He'd looked at her when she'd stepped back into the corner. "If this will keep the peace, then this is how it has to be for now."

Rick turned stone-faced and said nothing.

With her eyes, she begged for him to understand. This was for the best. For now.

The guard pressed the muzzle of his weapon against Rick's ribs. "You want me to tie him up?"

"Absolutely," Kemp said. "Find him a cot and secure everything. Don't trust him for a second."

"I won't," the guard said, and ushered Rick through the door.

Before he exited, Rick gave her one last glance, regret and overwhelming concern flooding his eyes. It took her breath away even though she knew he'd show care and concern for anyone in this situation. She told herself that, and yet there was something else in his eyes. Didn't he understand she didn't want to leave him? It had taken everything in her to willingly step away from Rick and go to Kemp.

Then the door shut, and Shay was left alone with the man behind all their troubles.

"Now what?" she asked.

"I'll take you to your quarters and let you get some rest, too." He raked a hand down his scruffy jowls and looked at her with tired red eyes. "When the time is right, I'll need you to fix that plane."

"And then we'll all just fly away together like one happy family, right?"

"I like your spirit." He grinned, but his eyes remained guarded, hiding the truth.

He opened the door and Shay grabbed her coat and stepped through, taking note that he hadn't exactly answered her question. But she didn't need him to. She knew how this was going to end if she and Rick couldn't get an advantage.

She walked with Kemp across the dried mud hole called a gold-mining camp toward the main house, which he explained served as his personal quarters. He went on again about keeping her safe from the men in the camp who'd been here for weeks without companionship. Though he claimed he'd protect her, a chill that wasn't from the Alaskan climate ran over her. She wrapped her arms around herself.

As they walked, men paused from whatever they were working on to watch her. She hated that. Hated that they knew exactly where she was going. Where she would stay. Probably tied up and helpless like Rick. Hated they would know where to find her in the night.

When she shuddered, Kemp slid a glance her way. "You ever been to Alaska before?"

"No. This is a first."

"This isn't cold. If you're lucky, you won't be here to experience the cold. I don't plan to be here, either."

Kemp unlocked the door to his mining-camp home. Strange that he'd keep it locked when there was no one here but his fellow workers. That told her more about their situation and his relationship with these men. He'd said that he'd protect her, and she knew that Rick would do whatever he could to keep her safe, but she had an eerie feeling that when it came down to it, she was on her own. Her father had tried to prepare her to be self-sufficient, to protect herself.

But would it be enough?

Rick woke up to a pounding headache. He wanted to find a new position on the cot but he'd been restrained and couldn't. Anger and frustration boiled inside.

Being held captive by a bunch of crazy men after gold went beyond ridiculous. That Aiden was still unaccounted for unsettled him, but even worse was being separated from Shay. Kemp claimed he'd protect her, but Rick didn't trust Kemp with her, either.

He wasn't any better.

An ache crawled over Rick's heart when he remembered the moment Shay had stepped from him to Kemp. He understood why she'd decided to pacify their keeper, but underneath the logic, Rick was afraid her actions meant that Shay couldn't really trust Rick. And under ordinary circumstances, he didn't want her to. He didn't deserve her, and she certainly didn't deserve a man she couldn't trust with her life.

A man she couldn't trust in her sleep, or rather in *his* sleep.

But right now their circumstances were anything but ordinary, and he needed them to be on the same page.

He was in the bunkhouse, where several of the men kept their belongings and cots. To get in as much work as possible before winter hit, they apparently worked around the clock and slept in shifts. There were sleeping forms in two of the cots around him—off-duty men grabbing their shut-eye.

The cot squeaked as Rick tried to find a comfortable position. Impossible. The space heater kicked in with a low hum, blocking out the backhoe and generator noises and the soft snores of the other two in the room.

Rick turned his thoughts to an escape plan.

He'd need to work the mining camp as if it were a reconnaissance mission. Obtain information—everything he could gather about his enemy through visual and any other methods. Survey the geography.

Something Kemp had said kept playing through his thoughts. *We're running out of time.*

The man clearly wanted the plane fixed in a hurry. That meant that Rick had maybe a day to figure things out, if that. Somehow he'd have to communicate his plans to Shay and pray she didn't go to Kemp for his protection. Rick growled under his breath and tossed in the cot, only to have his arms nearly jerked from their sockets. He had to shove her face from his thoughts or he'd never get any rest.

Sometime later pain shot through his side and Rick woke up. A foul-breathed grizzly of a man stood over him, jabbing him with his weapon. "Who can get any sleep around here with you?"

He tried to sit up but couldn't. "What do you mean?"

"You were screaming. Yelling at people. All in your sleep."

Rick said nothing as the guy eyed him suspiciously. The others in the bunkhouse groaned, and most got up and dressed. Rick wanted to scrape his hand down his face but couldn't. How long had he slept? Sunlight didn't slip through cracks in the shades and the cots were filled with men.

"Sorry," Rick finally said, but a small smile slid onto his lips. If they were exhausted, that could only help him.

"Do it again and I'll silence you." The younger of the men—the one who'd given him the medical kit—tugged on his knit cap, grabbed a weapon and left the bunkhouse along with the rest, except for grizzly man.

"You might as well cut me loose," Rick said. "I can't sleep, either."

"I could care less if you sleep."

"Come on, man," Rick said. "Let me sit in a chair with my hands tied—anything but this."

The guy scowled at Rick, but to Rick's surprise, he flipped open his knife to cut Rick free.

He was halfway done when a scream ripped through the night.

A woman's scream.

The man paused, but he had already cut enough of the plastic ties for Rick to twist his way free of the rest. Rick bulldozed over him, pounding him in the head until he was unconscious. He tore the weapon from the man's grasp, grabbed another man's coat and knit cap and bounded for the door.

Running through the camp armed like this might earn him a death sentence. Rick didn't care.

Shay. I have to get to Shay.

As he raced across the way to the main house along with a couple of others, he knew this wasn't at all the way he'd planned to make an escape. It wasn't a plan at all.

He just wanted to get to Shay.

God, please let her be okay.

Almost there.

He pumped his arms, running faster than the others.

He tried to rush through the door but it was locked. Rick pounded on the steel frame. "Let us in. Shay!"

He'd definitely earned that death sentence from the guard he'd pulverized. He would likely be chained like a dog from now on. But he could deal with it once he saw that Shay was safe. He heard someone fumbling with the locks from the other side. So much for Kemp's plan to protect Shay.

Rick had a split second to make a decision. He handed his weapon off to the armed man next to him. "Here, take this."

The guy's eyes widened in surprise but he had no time to react.

Red faced, Kemp swung open the door, light from the room behind illuminating the blood on his hands.

ELEVEN

"Shay!" Rick shoved Kemp out of the way and stepped into the small sparsely furnished living room. "Where is she?" He ground out the words.

"Rick?" Shay's voice sounded shaky. If Kemp so much as touched her, Rick was going to make him pay.

Ignoring the shouts behind him and the risk of being shot to death, he raced across the small space and down a short hallway. "Where are you?"

"In here." She appeared in a doorjamb, her face ashen and her hair askew. When she saw him, her mouth fell open and she rushed to him.

Relief swept over him when he didn't see any blood. But where had it come from?

He held her close, feeling her body tremble. "What happened? Are you okay?"

"Go find him!" From somewhere behind him, Kemp shouted orders at the men he held marginal control over.

Find who? They were running out of time in more ways than one. He could sense Kemp's fragile command slipping away.

The way Shay shook against him, he thought she might be sobbing. Rick had never been good at comforting anyone, but he had to try. He lifted his hand, hesitating before brushing it down her back. "Shh. It's going to be okay."

He heard Kemp's breathing the moment he came up behind him. Rick turned his face to the side, sending a lethal glare Kemp's way. "What happened?"

Kemp appeared almost as shaken as Shay and shook his head. He went into the bathroom. Rick heard the water running. Probably washing the blood from his hands.

Shay pulled away from Rick and stood on her toes to whisper in his ear. "Get me out of here." Anguish choked her hushed words. "Get us out."

Rick tugged her close and squeezed his eyes shut. "Soon," he whispered back.

Shay stepped away and wiped her eyes.

"Are you hurt?"

She shook her head.

Kemp stepped from the bathroom, wiped his hands on a towel and looked at Rick.

"Someone want to tell me what happened?" It hit Rick that he was alone in this house with Kemp, who wasn't holding a weapon. The guy had told his goons to go after someone. Someone who wasn't Rick. He could overpower him here and now.

But he still didn't know where Aiden was or how to get out of the camp safely. Escape would have to wait for now.

"A man came through the window," Shay said. "Into the room where Kemp put me. I screamed and then Kemp came through the door and fought the man. Stabbed him."

"He got away," Kemp said. "But he won't get far."

"This is exactly what I was afraid of." Rick left the confined space of the hallway and paced the living room.

Kemp followed. "For a second I thought it was you, breaking her out. Trying to escape."

"So it was one of *your* men? Someone you're ordering around?" Rick didn't need to ask why the man came for Shay. These unscrupulous men had been here for weeks without female companionship, it would seem.

"Yes." Kemp made his way to the kitchen. Rick's gun rested on the counter. Kemp quickly pressed his hand over it and chambered a round, sweat beading his brow. "At this rate, there won't be anyone left to work the mine. Add to that, someone is going to ask why I tried to kill one of my own men while protecting you. I don't know how much longer I can keep you alive. You need to fix the plane. I need to find the gold. Timing is going to be tricky."

He swiped the sweat away.

Shay moved to stand next to Rick. He swept her into his arms and held her close as if it was the most natural thing in the world. She didn't resist. Shay, the woman he'd considered strong and tough enough to walk the path she'd chosen, *needed* him right now. She was beyond vulnerable in this mining camp, and his own need to protect her was quickly growing into a driving force. If he it let it, it could drive him to make mistakes; it could drown out all reason. And in the end, that was no protection at all.

For a fleeting moment he wished he could have something with her once they were home again. But he couldn't spare the time to think about the future. The present needed all of his concentration.

"You don't need us. Let Shay fix the plane now and then let us go. Let my brother go before more people get hurt."

"I've lost two able bodies in a few hours. You're going to work and you'd better hope you can prove you have value. What can you do?"

Though he hated letting go, Rick released Shay. He strode to the counter and pressed his hands against it, reining in what he really wanted to do and say to this man. "You can't seriously think those henchmen are going to let me work alongside them. In fact, I'm thinking you might see an uprising before the day's out. They're getting restless."

"Don't you think I know that?" Kemp was getting restless, too.

Losing control. He likely wouldn't outlast, maybe wouldn't even outlive, this situation of his own creation.

"Why do they need you anyway?" Risk asked, pressing his point. "They can just take the gold for themselves once they find it."

Pouring on the doubt could destabilize the situation further. That would make things more dangerous, sure, but it could give them a chance to get away if the men were focused on other things.

"I'm the only experienced miner here. They have a job to do and that's to follow my orders. In the end, they might answer to someone else, but they've been instructed to obey each and every one of my orders. I could tell them to sit. Fetch. Roll over. And they'd obey like a good German shepherd. I could tell them to kill you or not. It's my call. So you'd better shut your mouth before I shut it for you."

Good. Rick was getting to him. Kemp was bluffing now. He'd already admitted that he was losing his persuasive power over the men where Rick, Shay and Aiden were concerned. "The only thing we can do is get in the way. Just let us go." Voicing his thoughts was a risk—if Kemp agreed that they'd only get in the way, then he might choose to eliminate them himself—but he didn't think Kemp was ready to dispose of them yet.

"Okay. Walk on out of here. See how far you get. I look forward to the show. You can't get fifty yards without these men gunning you down. They'd track you down before you could get a safe distance. But you already know that. You already tried to get away, before you even knew you were being stalked."

Rick got a better sense of just how trapped Kemp was himself. That Kemp was admitting this to them wasn't a good sign.

Kemp looked at Shay now, his expression hard. "The only way out is the small four-seat passenger plane sitting on the airstrip. We could all fly that out—the four of us. But I have to find the gold first, or else I'll be running forever. You fix the plane—" he turned to glare at Rick "—and you help me get to the gold, and you'll get to walk away. That's the only chance you have of getting out of here alive."

He started fixing a pot of coffee. The man was

unbelievable, his emotions as unpredictable as the circumstances.

"Tell me where my brother is. Let me see him." Rick was done with the games.

Kemp frowned and gave a subtle nod. "Not until it's time to leave."

If the man was using Aiden to keep Rick here, then maybe he doubted his own words about the plane being the only escape. Unfortunately, Rick was beginning to believe that his brother was already dead.

How was he going to keep Shay alive?

Someone knocked on the door. Weapon in hand, Kemp left the coffeepot brewing to answer it.

Shay remained by Rick's side, hoping he couldn't tell how shaky she still was. The man who'd gained access through the bedroom window with plans to assault her had held her down, breathing in her face and informing her to keep completely quiet or he'd slice her into pieces. This he said while pointing a knife at her throat.

At first she wasn't able to breathe, much less scream or even respond to him. What a complete failure she was—she was unable to move under the weight of fear and panic. Under the weight of the sturdy man.

Then he was suddenly thrown from her as

Kemp attacked with more strength, more rage, than she'd thought him capable of. When her assailant went for the gun he'd tucked in his waistband, Kemp stabbed him. All Shay saw was blood when Kemp had pulled the knife away.

She'd screamed.

Oddly enough, it almost seemed as if the guy fled through the window because of her scream rather than because of facing off with Kemp. What would happen to him now?

When Kemp opened the door, Rick turned Shay to face him. He gently cupped her face with his palms.

"Are you okay?" The tenderness in his touch, in his eyes, surprised her.

She never wanted to need anyone, but hearing that simple question and seeing the concern in his expression, she knew she'd never needed anything more in her life than for him to stay by her side. And that left her stunned.

How could she need him so much?

It didn't matter. She couldn't let herself need him.

If they weren't here now and in this situation, he would never talk to her like this. Touch her in such a tender way. It was all wrong. Messed up. And she couldn't let herself feel anything for him. Couldn't let her heart go through the hurt.

In response to his question, she nodded, unable to smile.

"Of course you're not. I'm sorry, Shay. Sorry about all of this." He let his hands fall away from her face and wrapped a finger around a tendril of her short hair.

What was going through his mind?

"It was my idea to go with him. I didn't want you to get hurt over me," she said. "You don't need to be sorry. So stop blaming yourself." She edged away.

Kemp let one of the men inside and walked back to Shay. "We have a problem with the backhoe and these clowns can't seem to fix it," he said.

She frowned. Why was he looking at her?

"What's this got to do with us?" Rick asked.

"Time to work." Kemp rounded the counter and scraped a mug from the cabinet to pour some coffee. He grabbed three more. "Shay's a mechanic."

Shay thought he wanted to keep that part a secret so that the men wouldn't know that she could fix the broken plane. What was he playing at?

"You know how to fix things, right? People with that ability and training can fix just about anything with the right tools."

"Are you telling me you don't already have

a mechanic for all this equipment? How could you make it through the summer without one?"

"We had a mechanic, *had* being the operative word." Kemp scratched the back of his head, appearing to measure his words. "He didn't get along with a couple of the guys. I think someone shot him."

Shay gasped. "You *think?*"

"I heard the gunfire. But I didn't see the body. So I can't be sure. But he was also the medic. I hated to lose him."

Rick stared at Kemp. Shay's knees buckled.

Dread fell on her like a cold Alaskan night. What happened if she couldn't fix whatever the problem was? Would the men decide she didn't have any value, just as Kemp said? Shay glanced at Rick, searching for his help, for a way out.

"What sort of problem are we talking about, exactly?" she asked.

"I don't know. You'll have to look at it yourself."

Shay examined her shaky hands. How on earth would she work in this cold, hostile environment with deadly pressure bearing down on her? Trying to pull herself together, she thought back to when she first got the job working for Connor. She'd had to prove herself then. She'd had to shove aside her fear and doubts and be strong. Make those men believers. She'd just have to do it again. But this Alaska incident had shaken her to the core. Made her question who she was. What she wanted in life.

Made her see Rick a lot differently, too. She could almost understand why he held everything inside—how did anyone communicate a terrifying experience like this? Who could possibly understand what they'd been through?

"Tools." She pulled her gaze from her calloused, rough mechanic's hands and looked at Kemp. A stocky man stood behind him. "What have you got?" she asked.

"They're in the toolshed. I'll show you."

"And the manual." Shay cocked her head. "Please tell me you have that."

Kemp frowned. "I'll look for it. Get your coat. The weather's going to turn nasty in the next few days, maybe hours. There are two storm systems pushing through. We need to make hay."

While Kemp ushered the man out the door, Shay headed for the bedroom, but Rick grabbed her arm. "What are you doing? You don't have to do this."

"Don't I? I think Kemp made it clear that the men are having second thoughts about our presence here. This is my chance to show them I have value. Besides, I thought that was the plan. To work while we figure out our escape. To find the gold so we can leave."

"I didn't mean for the pressure to fall on you. I don't want you to be the center..." Rick let his words trail off, his expression grim.

"Of attention," Shay finished. "You don't want me to be in the middle of conflict if it turns out that I can't fix the backhoe and there isn't any more digging for gold. I understand the risk, but the way I see it, if I don't fix it, we're in trouble. And as far as I've seen, I'm the center of attention anyway."

Creases ran across his forehead, between his brows. "Don't worry. I'll help you. I'll be right there by your side."

For the first time in hours, Shay felt the hint of a smile spread over her lips. "If there's one thing I'm confident about, it's my own abilities as a mechanic. If this thing is fixable, if we don't have to order a part, then I can handle it. What I can't handle are the guns. I can't work if I think there's a chance someone will point one at me. That would make anyone a little nervous." Even if they didn't have Shay's experiences, and those were beginning to rack up.

At her last words, Shay's smile fell and the creases in Rick's forehead deepened. Bringing up that incident hadn't been her intention. It seemed as if it would always stand between them, though.

After she'd watched her mother gunned down,

her father had made sure she knew how to protect herself. Carrying a weapon and protecting herself was one thing; being surrounded by miscreants who were eager to shoot to kill was another.

Even if she fixed the backhoe, Shay wasn't sure these men would let them see another day.

TWELVE

After visiting the shed full of rusty wrenches and other tools, Shay followed Kemp and his henchman to the broken excavator. There was a chill in the air that warned of a September storm. Whether it was accompanied by rain or snow didn't matter; Shay wasn't ready for colder temperatures.

As she marched with Kemp to the backhoe used for excavating the site, she grew ever conscious that all the men had stopped their work to watch her and to smile or tip their caps—or send her looks no woman wanted.

Shay opened the manual Kemp had found for her and tried to concentrate on that while she walked. It didn't work. Thank goodness Rick was beside her, and this time he wasn't even bound at the wrists. They were going to put him to work, too, knowing he'd comply with her life and Aiden's in the balance. Doing what, she didn't know. How long did it take someone to learn how to operate a backhoe? Weeks? Months? But she supposed there was plenty of other hard, backbreaking labor.

She understood better, too, why they weren't overly concerned about an escape. Escape to what? Kemp was right in that these men could gun them down and would consider it sport to hunt them if they left. And even if they got away from camp, where would they go? Any sign of civilization was miles away through wilderness that would be difficult to handle even with proper supplies and cold-weather gear.

That was why that airplane was the only way out of here. Their only chance. And she hadn't gotten her hands on it to fix it yet.

A couple of the men leaned against the boom part of the backhoe, blocking her path. When Kemp stepped aside, they held a challenge in their eyes, and something else that Shay didn't want to think about.

"Give her some room to work, will you?" Kemp growled.

He was right in guessing she'd probably be able to figure this out. She'd already been informed the loader wasn't working correctly. Shay glanced through the manual again. Of course, she knew about hydraulics. Pistons required oil to transmit the force between them.

She'd brought a few tools and a container for catching the hydraulic fluid.

"Let me see it in action. Somebody get this thing moving."

One of the men climbed onto the machine and started the ignition. The diesel fumes hit the air again along with a rattling noise. Shay cocked her head and listened. The rattling noise wasn't why she'd been called over to fix the thing, but it did signal that something else was wrong. She'd address that next. The backhoe operator worked the machine, or tried to, and Shay saw the problem with one of the pistons. She waved the operator down. He cut the ignition.

Sucking in a breath, she positioned the container to catch the hydraulic fluid, knowing she'd have to recycle that and use it again. Then she tried to grab a pair of needle-nose pliers. They slipped out of her shaking, sweat-damp hands. The men hovering around her made her too nervous to be steady.

Inhale…. She had to breathe….

Shay closed her eyes and imagined herself in the Deep Horizon hangar, working on their planes. The sounds were similar—men's voices, laughing. Jesting. But then a cold drop hit her face and she opened her eyes to reality.

She was in Alaska. The sky was getting ready to dump icy moisture in one form or another.

That served as a bitter slap to her face, and Shay thrust every other thought out of her mind while she worked. If anything, she needed to prove herself valuable.

It took her just over an hour, but when she finished repairing the piston, she climbed up into the seat of the backhoe. An image popped into her head of her simply rolling over all the bad guys. Of her and Rick and Aiden escaping. Too bad it wasn't that simple.

She caught a glimpse of Rick shoveling dirt to be carted to the trommel, which would break down the dirt into the smallest particles so the gold flecks could be retrieved. She knew because Kemp had gone on and on about his operation last night before she'd finally been left to rest. Rick paused and wiped sweat from his brow.

When Kemp had threatened to hurt her or Aiden if Rick didn't comply, she almost thought she heard in his voice that he thought Rick cared about her in a much deeper way. It was probably nothing more than her pathetic imaginings. But she had a feeling something between them had shifted. If Rick ever actually cared about her like that, could she maintain her distance? Could she protect her heart? Could she forget about that afternoon in the office?

Too many questions. She had to focus. Right

now she needed to test her work, and for that she'd need the backhoe operator again, who'd wandered off. In the meantime, she could listen to the engine again. Shay started the backhoe and the diesel engine roared to life. There was that rattle again that shouldn't be there. She didn't know what was causing it, but she was pretty sure she could fix it. Before she climbed down, she looked at Rick and saw him watching. Even from this distance, he looked as though he was admiring her, and warmth spread through her insides.

Rick is not the man for you.

He had too many issues. Just like her father. They were all stopped up inside of him.

Grimacing, Shay climbed from the enclosed cab and lifted the hood to see the air filter, radiator and oil. She went through a checklist of the basics but couldn't find the problem—and her fingers were growing numb. The temperature was slowly dropping.

She cupped her hands over her mouth, blowing her warm breath on them and rubbing them together. She wished there were a way she could work with gloves on, but her fingers felt too thick when she did that.

Regardless, her numb fingers had grown clumsy, and they slipped on a jagged edge, cutting her thumb open. She sucked in a hiss and jerked up, bumping her head on the hood. She hadn't finished the job. She had to finish, or they would think she wasn't worth keeping. And if that happened, it wouldn't be just her life on the line. Rick and Aiden were counting on her, too.

"Aiden." She huffed his name under her breath. Was he even still alive?

Shay squeezed her thumb, wiping the blood on the rag, and tightened a few loose bolts. Something anyone could have done if they'd had a mind to. Maybe that would take care of the rattling noise.

Stepping down, she sat on the step between the front and rear wheel, where she'd laid a few of the tools. A shadow fell over her, turning the gray skies even darker. Shay looked up to see a man staring down at her.

Joey.

He had the submachine gun hung across him. He was one of the men who guarded instead of working the mine.

His lips slid into a nasty smirk. "I've never seen a woman mechanic before. Was betting you couldn't do the job. I see you're proving me right."

For a moment, Shay sat frozen, unable to move, as if his stare had staked her to the spot. What was the matter with her? She forced herself to move. Without taking her eyes from him, she rose to her feet and stepped down to the ground. She slapped a wrench to his chest and he grabbed it without thinking.

"I get paid a lot more to do my job than you do to do yours." She climbed atop the tractor, wondering why she'd chosen those particular words.

She turned the key and the backhoe roared to life. Staring at the levers to operate it, Shay swallowed down her nerves. This could be a big mistake. She didn't have a clue what she was doing, but she had to try to prove she'd done her job. On a hunch, she grabbed the two joysticks and started moving the three joints of the backhoe as she'd move her shoulder, elbow and wrist. The arm of the backhoe moved just as she'd intended. Her repairs had worked as she'd known they would.

Shay looked down at the man with a triumphant grin. Others around the camp stopped what they were doing to look at the backhoe.

A shout rang out across the camp.

She'd just put the band of criminals back in business and bought her and Rick another day. Maybe.

While digging and transporting dirt to the trommel, Rick had made good use of his time keeping an eye on Shay but also taking in everything else. His focus was split between watching the men and scanning the buildings, looking for any sign of where Aiden might be kept. Doubts snaked through his core that his brother was even still alive.

Shay smiled on top of the backhoe—she must be relieved she'd gotten that piece of heavy machinery to work again. He was relieved, too. Things could have turned extremely nasty, and fast, otherwise.

He'd told her he'd be right there to help her, but Kemp had had other ideas, and Rick was powerless to change his mind about anything. The man was beginning to believe they were going to dig up enough gold in this one season to get him out of the debt he owed. The desperate search for riches clouded his judgment.

When Shay hopped down from the excavator, she snagged Rick's thoughts and held on. Longing coursed through him. He scraped his cold-numbed fingers through his hair. He allowed himself to really look at her. He already knew she was an extremely attractive woman both inside and out, as beautiful as she was strong.

Pulling his gaze from her, Rick thrust the shovel into the ground. She was and would always be off-limits to him. In the past, he'd made sure he didn't look beyond that tough veneer she kept in place, but their current predicament made that difficult. Things were best left the

vay they'd always been. He didn't trust him-
elf enough; why would Shay? Especially after
vhat he'd put her through, nearly pulling the
rigger. He hadn't realized he wasn't in the des-
rt surrounded by the enemy until it was almost
oo late.

No. Shay, or any woman, for that matter, was
ff-limits. But in this place—the absolute worst
lace for her—he was losing control over his
eart and mind. A severe need to protect her,
ave her and even be her hero scrambled his
houghts. He wasn't fit to be anyone's hero as
ong as he struggled with this problem he hadn't
ven wanted to admit that he had. No one knew
bout it—that is, except for Shay. Rick paused at
1e realization—and that made him feel closer
o her than to any other person in the world.

Closer to her than to his brother.

Shay *knew*.... She didn't know the circum-
tances, didn't know why he struggled with
ightmares he couldn't escape, but she knew
ow they affected him. And now he had new
odder for those nightmares.

She was here because of him. He'd let it hap-
en. Once again, he was incapacitated, made to
vatch helplessly as others got hurt—others he
vas supposed to protect.

Rick looked up at the gray sky, freezing rain
issing his cheeks.

Why, God?
Why do I have to go through this again?

The sky seemed to struggle with a decision o
whether or not to completely dump its contents
What would that do to this group of men, if they
were cooped up together indoors with nothing
to keep them occupied for too long? They'd kil
each other, that was what.

He would face off with Kemp as soon as he
got the chance. They needed to have a serious
conversation about what was going to happen i
these men didn't find the gold they were crav-
ing. What would happen, then, to him and Shay'

If Shay was going to fix the plane, it needed
to be soon. And if Rick had his way, the only
passengers on that flight out would be him, hi.
brother and Shay. He'd have to see how it played
out and could only hope they could fly out o
trouble in the near future.

With that thought, Rick glanced up to scan
the camp.

Reconnaissance.

If the plan to fix the plane didn't work
what then? There was also the problem that he
couldn't leave without Aiden.

*Where are you, Aiden? Where would he keep
you?*

That is, if his brother was even still alive.

THIRTEEN

Rick sat atop the backhoe, maneuvering the joystick levers to dig dirt and dump it in a pile. The skill had taken him several hours to grasp and he was still way too clumsy. To be worthy of his hire, it would take him weeks to master this. But thankfully they were too short handed to be picky about his abilities. Regardless of his haphazard maneuvering, the dirt would end up in the jig that pretty much automated the panning-for-gold process.

Though gray skies loomed, the full brunt of the storm held off, only teasing them with cold sprinkles and threatening them with more. So they continued to work through the afternoon.

The smell of diesel that fueled the excavator sent his mind back to his time in Afghanistan, to military caravans on backcountry desert roads. His thoughts hovered over the vicious fighting he'd witnessed and participated in as part of his job. You either grew numb in order to survive or your senses were heightened to every sound. Every smell. You turned to God, as had been his case, or you turned to something else. At first Aiden had chosen the bottle.

With the men standing around him, a few of them controlling the others with their weapons, he could almost imagine he was in a war zone. He had the sense that these men had shut themselves off from feeling. There was no sympathy to appeal to, no hope that he could convince one of the men to help him. He and Shay were on their own in a situation that was only a step away from descending into pure chaos.

Though the men didn't tell him much, he'd learned that they were bringing in only a few ounces of gold a day, and Kemp had had to cash in that gold to keep the operation going.

But gold flakes or pieces weren't like the nuggets Kemp had supposedly promised the man he owed.

Rick watched Shay over at the shaker wash pan helping another guy clean it out. He hated that Kemp had kept them separated like this, but tonight he would insist they stay together so he could protect her. Kemp had all the proof he needed after last night's assault that Shay wasn't safe on her own. And what about his brother? Was Aiden safe, wherever it was they'd stashed him?

He watched every man, guarding or working, to see if anyone disappeared or went with a plate of food to one of the buildings where Aiden might be kept. But he saw nothing.

His stomach growled. It had to cost a small fortune to keep these men fed. The crack of a rifle rang out in the distance and Rick stiffened, all his senses on alert.

He reminded himself that he wasn't in the Middle East now. He wasn't a marine anymore. He shoved his focus back to digging dirt, watching the camp and forming an escape plan in case plan A involving the airplane didn't work.

An hour later, he spotted one of the men hauling in a four-point buck.

Rick's mouth watered at the thought of venison. What was he doing? He couldn't just settle into this life. For that matter, none of them could.

At the evening meal, the men washed up and sat at the table in the mess hall, the aroma of venison wafting over them. A guard nudged Rick from behind with his gun as he grabbed his plate of food, reminding him that his time was short.

His, Shay's and Aiden's time was short. The

men were growing restless, just as Kemp had said they were. Rick's gut churned. Kemp was playing them all.

He plopped next to Kemp and ate quietly, Shay sitting across from him. Though she appeared exhausted, the work seemed to have exhilarated her. He knew it had to be better than being held somewhere, captive and bound.

When the guy next to him finished his meal and left the table, Rick leaned close to Kemp. "We need to talk."

Kemp dug into his baked beans as if he hadn't heard Rick. Then he suddenly dropped his fork against the plate and jumped up. Grabbing his dish, he tossed it in the sink with a bang.

Rick had no doubt that juggling his own agenda, his accidental captives and the nonproducing mine was wearing on him. The problem was, Kemp carried a huge burden. Rick knew only too well what that could do to a man.

Kemp was going to explode, and soon. Rick just hoped the people he cared about most in the world were out of harm's way when it happened. A pang went through his heart at the thought.

Picking his teeth with a toothpick, Kemp never once looked at Rick, who'd now lost his own appetite. He glanced at Shay, her face ashen, the color brought by the day's work drained.

"Give us a minute," Kemp said to the guard and other worker who'd remained inside.

The guard frowned at Kemp. "You sure about that?"

"Bind him, then. Toss me your weapon."

It was Rick's turn to frown, but if having his hands tied was the price for getting a minute with the crazy man running this operation, then so be it.

While the guard bound his wrists in plastic ties for not the first time—his ankles, too—he thought about Shay. He watched her sullen features as he was being strapped to the chair, made to feel completely powerless. Impotent.

Shay.

They hadn't been bound that morning while in Kemp's quarters, but the man had something to prove now.

And Rick had to protect Shay. Not only from these men and this situation but from himself. He tore his gaze from her to slice Kemp open with his glare. The guard clomped out of the kitchen.

"The men are talking amongst themselves. They don't hold back in front of me because they think you're going to kill me anyway. Either that or they will. So they don't care what I know. But they're getting restless. The claim isn't bringing the gold you promised."

Kemp pulled up a chair to face Rick. "Is that it? That's what you wanted to talk about? Tell me something I don't know."

"No. *You* tell *me*." Rick ground out the words. Fear crept into Kemp's gaze despite Rick's bound position. "I want to know your plan. What's going to happen when these men become certain that they aren't going to find the gold they were expecting? When are you going to let Shay fix the plane and let us get out of here?"

Chewing on his toothpick, Kemp waited before he answered. Almost as though he wanted Rick to remember who was in charge. But it was too late. Rick had seen the fear in his eyes. The man was near the breaking point.

"There's another storm headed this way. Not a rainstorm but snow this time. So a few of the men are leaving tomorrow to get some supplies we ordered before it gets too difficult to leave the area," Kemp said. "That'll take them half the morning. I'll take her to the strip then. But you're staying here."

"No," Shay said. "Rick is coming, too. I need his help. He helps me fix the plane at the place we work."

At most, he'd handed her a wrench a time or two—but Rick certainly wasn't going to contradict her. Shay glanced at him, never giving away the truth. He flooded his gaze with approval.

Her eyes crinkled around the corners just a little. Just enough for Rick to notice.

"You try anything and you won't see your brother alive. Understand? You try anything and I just might kill the both of you right then and there."

The wariness in his eyes told Rick he meant his words. And behind his gaze, Rick saw confirmation of another truth—Kemp would most likely leave them behind anyway, dead or alive.

"Understood," Rick said. "We want to get out of here in one piece, just like you. Why can't you let me see my brother now? See that you're taking care of him. That he's alive."

"Maybe tomorrow."

Rick couldn't allow himself to hope. Kemp took pleasure in toying with him. Enjoyed the game too much. Rick let the point drop and focused on his other goal. "And for tonight I need to be with Shay. Make sure she's protected. I don't trust anyone else. You saw what happened last night."

"That's fine by me, but both of you will be bound." He looked at Shay for her agreement. She could choose to stay with Kemp and have the freedom to move about in the room where he locked her or remain bound with Rick.

"How can I protect her, then, if someone tries—"

"They won't."

Rick didn't like this arrangement, either. "What happened to the guy you stabbed, anyway? Did he get away?"

"Found him dead in the woods. I didn't kill him. Animals got to him. Wolves, maybe."

Rick closed his eyes, wishing he could drive away the image that appeared. Just another one to add to his bad dreams. At least if he was bound tonight and fell asleep, he couldn't harm Shay if nightmares accosted him.

Funny that he'd wanted to be with her to protect her when he had to protect her from himself, as well.

Rick sat in an uncomfortable hard-backed chair that was nailed to the floor. They'd bound him to the chair as promised, after he'd been allowed to clean up. Kemp wouldn't have them in the main house smelling of the outdoors, mud and dirt. Rick didn't understand why he cared.

They were both so exhausted that neither of them had spoken much once they'd been placed in the small windowless room in Kemp's main house. He'd left a small lamp on in the room so they could see, but it wasn't as if they were going to trip or stumble in the dark. Tied up like this, they weren't going anywhere.

Rick wondered if Shay regretted agreeing to

out completely. Then, if Shay fixed the plane, they could simply take off. But he doubted Kemp would let himself be caught off guard like that.

And if either of those plans failed, Rick was out of options. He felt as helpless as he'd been in Afghanistan—a forgotten place in many American homes.

He watched Shay, listening to the wind blow through the cracks of the house. His lids grew heavy, but he fought the need to sleep. Nothing good would come of him falling asleep.

His Cobra helicopter whirled in the sky— warning signals resounding all around him. The helicopter crash-landed, skidding into a sand- bank. Rick crawled from the ruins and dragged his copilot away from the burning wreckage. They needed to make it to shelter, where Rick could assess the situation. Where they could hide until help came. Rick scanned the area and made a decision. He started for a building across the street.

A bomb exploded from the building.

The concussive force of the blast, the shock wave of air pressure, sent Rick flying through the air. His ears rang, deafening him to all other sounds as he lay on the ground, only vaguely aware of the pain. Only partially conscious. But he wouldn't give in to the urge to lie still. He dragged himself to his feet and searched for his copilot, his friend—he had to get him to the cover of another building not ten yards away.

Ten long yards.

Automatic weapons spewed bullets around him.

"No!"

FOURTEEN

Shay jerked awake. She fought the confusion shrouding her.

Where am I?

Rick's groaning form in the chair over in the corner caught her attention and quickly re-oriented her. One tug of her hands reminded her that she was bound in place.

Rick moaned again, his forehead creased in anguish, and then he cried out. That sent Shay right back to the day in the office when she'd tried to wake him up. Only then, he'd had free range of motion and a weapon to protect himself from whatever evil tortured him in his dreams.

He didn't have anything to protect himself with today. "Rick," she said. "Rick, wake up."

His head bobbed and rolled and then his eyes slowly slid open and found her. "Shay," he whispered. Relief swept through his gaze.

"You were dreaming." More like having a nightmare. What haunted him so?

He blinked and cleared his throat, throwing off the vestiges of a not-so-peaceful slumber.

"I'm sorry," he said, closing his eyes again.

Shay had the feeling he didn't want to look at her. "What do you have to be sorry about?"

His lids slid open again. "I wasn't supposed to fall asleep. Did I wake you?"

Shay gave him a soft smile in answer. "I don't even remember falling asleep."

"No one ever does." Rick tried to smile, but the anguish she'd heard in his groans resided behind his gaze.

"Tell me about your dreams." *The* dream. She should have said *the* dream. She knew he'd had this one before. A deep sadness dropped into her heart, but she knew that Rick Savage would not appreciate pity. And she didn't pity him. Not really.

What she felt for Rick… It scared her. She couldn't face it. This wasn't the time.

Tears threatened behind her eyes. She hated them. "I want to know, Rick. What…happened to you?"

She knew enough to understand that his nightmares had to be linked to his time overseas in the U.S. Marines. She'd heard him talk enough about his brother turning to alcohol in the aftermath of his own military experiences. And she knew that Rick had turned to God—she'd heard him talking about that with the other men at Deep Horizon. Had seen him pray. But had any of them seen him while he slept? Was God really there for him?

"You don't want to know, Shay."

"I think I deserve that much, don't you?"

His eyes held a kind of sorrow and regret. In his gaze she saw again how remorseful he was about that day when he'd nearly attacked her.

She could tell he struggled for the words. Maybe no words could ever explain what he'd gone through, but she pressed him anyway. "We don't know what we're going to be doing in a few hours. We might both be dead. Please, tell me…"

"I can't."

Rick held her gaze, nearly caressing her with his eyes. Her heart fluttered—did he really see her that way? He'd never really looked at her before this ordeal.

She wanted nothing more than to be free of these stupid plastic ties and go to him. Let him wrap his arms around her. Never in her life had she been so grateful to be tied up—Rick was dangerous to her heart, and maybe even dangerous to her physically. She needed the reminder not to get close to him, no matter how badly she wanted to. But even though she couldn't approach him physically, she still wanted to try to reach out to soothe the pain he was feeling.

"Okay. I'll go first. My father used to do that to me. After my mother died, he held everything bottled up inside him. She died when a man shot her. Right in front of me." Tears surged in her throat.

"I guess that makes what happened that day I aimed at you even more terrifying." He sighed, defeated.

"Yes. You have no idea. But after that, my father just closed himself off to everyone. Me and my sister? We needed him. But we couldn't seem to reach him. He couldn't see anything past the pain he was in. I could see he was like a soda bottle when you shake it, ready to burst."

"Then we understand each other. I can't afford to touch that cap. I wish I could. I'd do it for you, if I could."

"If you mean that, then let me in." *What are you doing? You can't risk your heart!*

"Why would you want in, Shay? You've already seen what I can be. I'm dangerous to anyone I might…"

Love? Shay's heart skipped erratically. She was edging closer to the danger zone she'd managed to keep a safe distance from all this time.

"Anyone I care about," he said, finishing his sentence.

"There are specialists out there to assist people who struggle with what you're going through.

Why don't you get help? Then you could have a relationship with someone." *Just not me.*

Rick surprised Shay with a smile. "And who would I have this relationship with, Shay?"

The way he looked at her, that little flirting glint, stirred her insides. Her pulse raced. No, she couldn't do this. She'd been guarding her heart for too long. Rick had been safe to think about because he'd never noticed her. She tugged her gaze from him and stared at the empty, boring wall, unable or unwilling to answer him.

But if she really didn't want the chance for a relationship with him, then why was she trying to get him to open up? He'd been safe before; now she was trying to open that soda-bottle cap so she could…what? Convince herself that it might be safe to love him after all?

Suddenly, Rick began straining against the chair, his face turning a little red.

"What are you doing?"

He moved his shoulders up and down and whipped his hands around in front of him. The motion looked odd, but to her astonishment, he eventually succeeded in freeing himself.

Shay gasped. "How did you do that? Why haven't you done that before? I don't understand."

"I learned a trick. Hold my wrists wide when they're tying me to give me a little slack to maneuver later. It doesn't always work. But it worked for me this time. I needed to get out of this." He began working on his ankles where they were tied to the chair. Not so easy, but nothing he couldn't handle. When he'd freed himself from the chair, he moved to Shay and worked on the ties until they came undone.

She rubbed her wrists and shook her arms out. How good it would feel to sleep in a normal position. To be back safely in her own bed. "What will they say when they find that we've freed ourselves?"

"Freed? We're still bolted into this room, in case you haven't noticed." Then he shrugged. "No one will even know, except for Kemp when he comes to let us out. And since Kemp needs you to fix the plane, he won't complain too much. So let's enjoy being moderately more comfortable while we make our plans."

Shay rubbed her arms and scooted over for Rick to sit next to her.

Rick dropped to the edge of the bed, acting restless. He reached over and pressed his palm tenderly against her cheek. "Shay, when we make it out of this…"

Shay leaned into the tenderness in his hand, closing her eyes. Despite all her resolve to wall off her emotions, she craved the gentle, caring touch from this man she'd admired from a distance for so long. Never had she dreamed he would look at her like this. Talk to her like this. Was she imagining this? And yet the safety net she'd placed around her heart was in jeopardy. Rick wasn't supposed to care about her.

I want to be free to love you....

The thought startled Rick, almost taking his breath away. He'd worked hard to hold himself in check when it came to this woman. He'd never allowed himself to look at her. And she'd never given him reason to. Until now. Until this situation wore away his defenses. Was he out of line even thinking like this?

Shay'd given him a small measure of hope.

Maybe...maybe she would love him back, if given the chance.

Her face resting against his hand, she kept her eyes closed as if she was soaking in his touch. He slid his thumb down her cheek, feeling the silkiness of her skin. She could simply be desperate for affection, the warmth of care and concern from another human being in this terrifying mining-camp prison. So he couldn't know if her reaction was really about him or about seeking whatever comfort she could find in their hopeless circumstances.

But she might very well be the one woman who could see him through. Who would stick with him. And, oh, Rick wanted that with her; he realized that now.

When she opened her eyes, which seemed to hold the beauty of Alaska within them, he let his hand drop away, watching her, searching her gaze. For what, he wasn't sure.

"I thought…" she whispered. "I thought you were safe…."

Unsure what she meant, he angled his head. "Safe?"

"After seeing how my father hurt, I never wanted to care about someone the way he cared about my mother. I thought you were safe to fall for because you never once looked—"

A noise on the other side of the door cut her off. The moment was lost, and they still hadn't discussed their plans for escape.

Time was up. He'd have to spit this out fast. "Listen, when you go to fix the plane, I'm going to distract Kemp. Watch for it. I want you to radio for help."

Her eyes grew wide. "But—"

The door swung open.

Rick stood to face the butt of an automatic weapon in his temple.

Pain sent blackness across his vision, fading in and out until finally, darkness engulfed him.

FIFTEEN

"No!" Shay screamed.

Rick fell to the floor.

Shay knelt next to his unconscious body, her concern over him trumping her fear of the guy with the gun.

Kemp appeared behind the man. "What have you done?"

"He hit him in the head for no reason." She forced her venom through clenched teeth. "Please, call your dog off."

Cradling Rick's head, she prayed he would be all right. "Please, wake up."

A knot swelled on his forehead.

"I didn't give you authority to hurt them."

"He was trying to escape," the man said. "I don't need your permission. You forget who you answer to."

Shay tried to slide Rick away from the two men. Their posture suggested that if the argument escalated, they might come to blows, or worse, guns. Kemp didn't hide his anger at the guard and got in his face.

"You're the one who's forgotten who you answer to. I'm in charge while you're here. I run the claim. Now back down before I make a call or get rid of you myself."

The man kicked Rick in the gut before he left the room. Brandishing his own weapon, Kemp scowled at the man when he passed. Once he was out of earshot, Kemp looked at her and frowned. "Never liked the guy."

"How can we fix the plane now?" she whispered.

"Looks like he won't be going." Kemp crossed his arms, his frown deepening as he looked down at Rick.

"I won't leave him. I can't fix the plane without him anyway," Shay said. "I need his help." To hold a wrench, maybe.

"Then you'd better make him wake up." He shoved Rick with his boot. "To tell you the truth, I would have hit him in the head myself if I'd been the one to open the door and see him untied. Maybe next time, I'll make sure he's restrained with something…more permanent."

Shay couldn't hold Kemp's insidious stare, and pressed her forehead against Rick's, careful not to touch the bruise. "Give him a few minutes to come to. We need some breakfast, too, okay?" Shay tried to steady her trembling voice.

"Half an hour. That's all. The next time I open this door, he'd better be cowering in the corner like he should have been to begin with."

Shay nodded, wanting to appease this man who controlled their fate. As long as she seemed to fall in line—and as long as he needed her help—there was a chance they were safe. As soon as she fixed that plane, all bets were off. Somehow she had to delay the repairs and yet make it so they could fly away at a moment's notice. Add to that, she wasn't certain she could even make the repairs so easily. Kemp hadn't said whether or not anyone had been able to find the replacement part in the remains of the Jeep. The pressure squeezed her chest. Too much was riding on her.

More so than yesterday, when she'd had to prove there was a reason for her to exist at the camp. Today she'd have to prove her worth, and secure their only escape.

Shay slid Rick's shoulders onto her lap and held his head, caressing his face. Why did her heart give her such fits where this man was concerned?

She'd often heard that girls ended up marrying a man like their father. Rick was just like her father. Both men had suffered through a traumatic experience. Both men held on to the anguish, tucking it deep inside. She hadn't been able to help her father. Would she be able to help Rick?

She'd never find out if he didn't wake up so they could get out of here.

"Rick, you have to wake up. I can't do this without you. Our plan won't work." If he wasn't there to distract Kemp, she couldn't make the call on the plane's radio.

He groaned.

Her heart leaped. She pressed her hands against his face. "Rick!"

His eyes fluttered opened. Squinting, he appeared to be a little dazed as he looked at her. Then his eyes seemed to focus and his hand slipped up to cup her cheek again, just like before. Again, his gaze caressed her face and slowed at her lips.

Her pulse ramped up. "Rick," she whispered. "Thank goodness, you're okay."

Rick lifted his other hand and in an instant pulled her close and pressed his lips gently against hers. "I am now," he said, his voice gruff.

His musky scent wrapped around her and for a fleeting moment, she didn't care about anything but him. The things that stood between them seemed to disappear. Even the fact that they were prisoners here drifted away.

The lock outside the door clinked. Rick released her and shoved to sit up. She could tell he was still a little shaky, but he stood to meet the new challenge. When the door opened this time, Rick had her pressed behind him against the wall.

Cowering in the corner?

No, that wasn't her Rick. Her Rick?

Kemp tossed them a couple of bottles of water and energy bars. "Eat up. Time's running short."

Rick took a step forward. "What about the guards? I thought they were here to guard you as much as us."

"Not that it's any of your business, but I told the guy left behind to stay on me that he could have whatever gold he uncovered from the wave table today. It's amazing what a few ounces of gold will do. Not bad earnings for one morning of work. Besides, he knows there's no way for me to escape." He closed the door.

Rick turned to face Shay. "I guess they don't see the airplane as any sort of threat since it's not in working condition. Kemp isn't a flight risk, as it were. They haven't figured out that you're actually an airplane mechanic."

Or had they? They knew she could fix machines—it wasn't that much of a stretch to wonder if she could fix airplanes, too. What would happen if the men caught on to their ruse?

Shay grabbed the water and tore into the bar She needed sustenance if she was going to make it through this day. "If we're discovered coming or going to the airplane, they'll destroy it. And if I fix it, Kemp won't need us anymore."

"Then don't fix it."

"What?"

"Not completely. Leave some reason that Kemp still needs us for a little while longer. If you can make the radio call, then we'll only have to stay alive long enough for help to come. Or long enough to escape ourselves."

Rick scarfed down the energy bar and guzzled the water. He tried to ignore the throb in his head. He'd had worse and knew how to deal with the pain. Shay lifted the bottle of water to her lips, her hands trembling.

Rick finished his off, then reached for her hands. He squeezed them in his, feeling her strength and softness there all in one hand. Just like Shay—she was the strongest woman he'd ever known, and yet she was soft, tender and caring at the same time. A person could be all those things, he knew. It was just that he'd never met someone who actually was all those things wrapped into one person. A person who was so beautiful. A person he couldn't stop think ing about, and not just because they were captives together.

"It's going to be all right. All you have to do is your job. Remember what you said about fixing the backhoe. You know how to do this. Leave everything else to me."

"But I have a feeling that this is it. That something is about to happen to us one way or the other to determine whether we can get out of here or not."

"Call for help, Shay. Fix the plane most of the way, and call for help. Don't think about anything else. In fact, don't worry about just fixing it partway. It'll be simpler if I don't just distract Kemp but take him down instead. That is, if you give me a signal that we can take off in the plane. If you can actually fix it."

Shay shook her head. "He's going to be expecting you to try. You can't risk it. I'm afraid for you. Besides, what about your brother?'

Rick sighed. "You're my first concern. Let me worry about my brother."

She'd always been his first concern. Had he known the danger they would face, had he expected it, prepared for it as he should have, she wouldn't be here now. He ran his thumb down her cheek again, warning sirens echoing with the pain in his head. But he couldn't just brush away the tenderness he felt for her, because this might be their last few moments together. He couldn't listen to the warnings signals that told him to protect his heart and hers.

Kemp brushed into the room. "Break it up. We have work to do."

Rick stepped away from Shay, experiencing a new wave of loathing for this man.

"Take a minute and use the facilities. Then let's go. The men who matter have left already to get supplies, but they won't be gone that long. My guard is working the claim for his own benefit, but don't be fooled—all the men left behind also carry guns. And they won't hesitate to use them."

Shay and Rick followed Kemp out the door of the pantry converted to a jail cell. Tension knotted Rick's neck with the same apprehension Shay was feeling. He, too, could sense that they were getting close to the end.

After using the facilities, they met in the kitchen.

Kemp faced them and chambered a round. "Don't think I won't be expecting you to try to take the plane today. So I brought you a note."

He pushed a slip of paper across the kitchen counter.

Rick stared at it, instantly recognizing the scrawl as his brother's. His pulse roared in his ears. Reaching over, he picked up the paper and read it. "Rick, please don't leave without me. Aiden."

Aiden wouldn't willingly write those words. Blood boiled across Rick's vision. He crumpled the paper in his fist. "Why, you..." He ground out the words, wanting nothing more than to get his hands around Kemp's throat and choke the whereabouts of his brother out of him.

The evil man smirked. "Thought that would keep you here. Remind you that your brother is counting on you. As soon as it's time, we'll get him, and then we'll leave and I'll drop you off somewhere safe."

And just why would he let them go? They'd seen his face. They'd seen everything. Why was Kemp dancing around the obvious? Rick considered asking him but thought better of it. No point in driving home the point, just in case the man was actually that delusional.

At least the note gave Rick hope—not certainty but hope—that Aiden was still alive. Still, he'd turn optimist like Shay, because he couldn't stand to think of Aiden as anything but alive.

If he got that chance to leave today, the questions still remained.

Should he save Shay and leave Aiden? Or wait to save him, too, but risk them all?

SIXTEEN

Carrying her tool set and the gasket she needed to fix the exhaust leak that Aiden had described, Shay tucked her hood over her head and stepped out into the cold, running over the repair she'd need to make in her head.

She had the gasket and hoped a simple replacement would fix the problem. But if Kemp hadn't flown the thing all this time and it was eroded too badly, it might require more than she could do here. That possibility had nagged her for days now. She'd buried those concerns, trying to stay optimistic, but maybe she should think like a realist. Like Rick.

What if she couldn't repair the plane in time? Or at all?

She calmed her breathing. She had to do this. *Please, God, let it be a simple fix.* She couldn't think of anything she wanted more at that moment than to fly away, even though she hated flying.

She sucked in the colder air brought in with the storm. Thank goodness it had blown through yesterday and had all but gone, leaving barely a dusting of snow that was quickly melting as the morning warmed up.

Any season in interior Alaska could be unpredictable, but the fall months leading into winter didn't leave room for any surprises. They should expect the unexpected. If for some insane reason they ended up stuck here for a few more weeks and Alaska turned brutal, the weather would be more than they could survive in the exposed setting of the mining camp. But who was she kidding? The men had no plans to stay that long—and no matter what happened, she was sure the men wouldn't willingly let her or Rick leave alive.

The camp seemed eerily quiet. No one worked the backhoe or the bulldozer. The jig was cranked up and running, but only a couple of men milled about in that area. The three of them—Rick, Shay and Kemp—easily slipped off behind the buildings and into the thick woods.

Kemp followed an overgrown trail, confident his note from Aiden would keep Rick in line. But Shay wasn't so sure. They were as free here as they'd been since arriving. Escape was almost within reach. In fact, she had no doubt that if she could fix the plane, Rick would try to overpower Kemp and get the upper hand. They would leave. But Kemp had driven a nail deep into Rick's heart, making it clear that any action from Rick could be used as an excuse to punish Aiden.

Aiden wasn't even her brother, and she couldn't see herself leaving without him now, if she ever could have.

They hiked up an incline, reminding her of just a few days earlier when she and Rick had made their way down into a gorge to get their things from the Jeep. Shay had had to face her fear of heights to make it—but Rick had been there with her, helping her all the way.

Oh, Rick.

He was quickly burrowing underneath her protective barrier. Shay almost felt helpless against his charm—charm she'd never dream would be directed her way. She'd certainly never imagined this particular scenario, either. Maybe that was the problem—she couldn't have known just what kind of protection she'd need, so she hadn't been able to defend herself against the way their situation had made her feelings impossible to ignore.

After a half-mile hike, Kemp pushed through the trees to the short landing strip. Over and out of the way was a rudimentary hangar, where he'd parked the plane. The shed offered meager protection. Shay would have to do much more than the part replacement to make sure the aircraft was even airworthy after being so exposed to the elements.

Kemp hurried across the airstrip to the plane, Shay and Rick on his heels, each of them seemingly preoccupied with their own agendas. Each of them well aware that the other men would return soon. Maybe before she'd completed her task. Maybe they'd even be discovered.

Shay set her toolbox and the gasket down and drew in a breath. Often at Deep Horizon's hangar, she had to shove all distractions aside in order to do her job. She was in her element now. Shay would get this baby flying.

And when she knew the plane was ready, she was supposed to signal Rick. They'd never really gotten to what the signal should be, but maybe a look and a nod would be enough for him. She and Rick had worked together, albeit at different jobs, for Deep Horizon for a couple of years now. She had a feeling he'd be able to tell when she finally got things up and running.

Rick remained at her side as she tried to start the plane and listen to the engine. Kemp stood near them, holding an intimidating posture. Ready to shoot for the slightest reason. She tried not to think about that, or else her limbs would shake even more than they already were.

Rick pressed a hand over hers to reassure her, but even that couldn't calm her nerves.

Aiden had been right—the problem appeared to be an exhaust leak. She climbed out of the cockpit and raised the hood.

She had to make it look as if she needed Rick to help her with this, or else he didn't have much value to Kemp other than leverage for Shay's cooperation. But Rick's nearness scrambled her thoughts on top of the pressure she already felt. Still, she managed to stammer out some instructions for simple tasks he could help her complete.

Time held no meaning as she worked. A good hour or more could have passed and she wouldn't have known. When she glanced up, she saw that Kemp had opened his satellite-phone case and was making a call.

When she finished installing the new gasket, she closed the hood and nodded at Rick. Kemp was deep in conversation, so she felt it safe to speak.

"I fixed the problem. There might be other maintenance issues, which I'll need to look at, and we'll need to do a preflight check. That'll take more time. You're not planning to leave without Aiden, are you?"

"He didn't write that note without coercion." He whispered so low she could barely hear him. "He wouldn't ever have said that."

"But don't you think he wants us to find him and take him with us?"

Frown lines cut deeper into his face. "Of course he does. If I were him, I'd want that, too, in a perfect world. I'd also want you to take the only chance you had and either come back for me later or trust me to find my own way out."

Rick swallowed. Shay could tell this was a struggle for him. She would make it easy. "For now, let's stay. Stick to the plan. I'll make the radio call."

He held her gaze and something passed between them. She was about to question him again when he turned and strolled over to Kemp, blocking his view of Shay. Good. This was her chance to make the call. They weren't going to leave Aiden.

She climbed into the cockpit. First she looked for the ELT—the emergency locator transmitter—to flip it on. That would send a signal that they needed help. Where was the thing? Didn't this plane have one?

She couldn't find it, so she turned her attention to the radio. Rick should be the one to do this. He'd know what to do. But he was also the better choice to distract Kemp. That meant Shay had to do this part. She drew in a few calming breaths, remembering the words Rick had told her to say.

She flipped on the radio and turned to the emergency frequency.

Nothing.

What? On and off, she flipped. The radio was dead.

Disappointment seized her. She had to let Rick know their plan was a complete failure. Not only had she been unable to make the radio call, she also didn't feel confident in taking the plane until she'd checked all the systems. She'd been afraid to start that process earlier because she didn't want Kemp to think she'd fixed the problem yet. She had to give him a reason to still need her. There was a tricky balance in gaining the advantage and maintaining control and she'd taken measures to make sure that happened.

From somewhere in the distance, Kemp shouted, "I'll kill you!"

Shay climbed from the cockpit. Rick had a stranglehold on Kemp. "Go ahead, Shay!" he yelled out. "Start the plane!"

Panic flooded her. She couldn't fly. Didn't he remember that she wasn't a pilot? She didn't know if the Cessna was even airworthy. And what about Aiden? All those thoughts raced through her mind at the same excruciating moment in time. Unfortunately, the thoughts kept her frozen, staring at the desperate struggle between Kemp and Rick.

If Rick didn't win this, they were both dead.

Veins bulged in Kemp's temple and his neck as he slowly forced the gun back at Rick's head, his finger on the trigger. She wouldn't have imagined he would be so strong.

She had to do something.

Shay stumbled forward. "No!"

"Start. The. Plane." Rick choked out the words. "Do it."

From where she stood, that didn't seem like a good plan.

If Kemp shot Rick, what did it matter if she could get the plane started or not? Shay ran toward the two men, preparing to wrestle the gun from Kemp and away from Rick's head. Both men turned red with exertion in their struggle for power and control. Rick pressed the weapon away from his head.

Kemp shifted against him and the gun went off.

Shay's heart ricocheted. "No..." she whimpered.

Rick...

He dropped to the ground.

This wasn't supposed to happen. It's not supposed to end this way.

Kemp caught his breath and aimed the weapon at Rick's face this time.

Shay screamed and ran toward him, shoving the weapon away just as it went off again, the resounding shock wave of gunfire ringing through her core.

Her ears still rang, but she didn't let that make her hesitate for another moment. "You kill him now and you won't leave," she yelled out. "I won't finish the repairs."

Kemp yanked her arm and twisted. He pressed the gun under her chin. "I told you if either of you tried anything, someone would get hurt. I'm thinking that someone might have to be you. What do you mean you won't finish? Didn't you already do that? If the plane is fixed, then I don't need you anymore."

Kemp had turned vicious.

"There's more wrong with it than just the part that needed replacing. You can't fly the plane out yet." Shay blinked away the sweat of fear from her eyes, grateful she'd thought ahead and made sure to disable it so he couldn't fly without her help.

"If you're lying, I'll forget the plane and kill you anyway."

Shay stared him down, forcing all the loathing she could into her gaze, but that didn't keep the tears from streaking down her cheeks. "I'm not lying, either, when I tell you that if you kill him, or if you let him die, I won't complete the repairs. You won't leave this place alive, either."

She forced bravado into her words, strength brought on by the image of this man shooting Rick. The man she couldn't love. The man she couldn't stop herself from loving, either.

Rick opened his eyes.

Fire burned across his shoulder and brought the images screaming back.

He'd tried to trick Kemp, knowing it would be a risky move. But he'd realized this would be their best chance, maybe even their only chance, to escape. He'd reconciled himself to the idea by promising himself he'd call for help in getting Aiden out, if Shay hadn't already done so, as soon as they got into the air.

But he'd underestimated Kemp and they'd struggled.

The gun had gone off.

That was all Rick remembered.

Shay's face appeared in his line of vision, her soft smile not entirely covering the frown.

"We have to stop meeting like this," he said with a chuckle. Though there was nothing funny about this. He was incapacitated. No use to anyone.

Again.

Why hadn't Kemp simply killed him?

He glanced around, his body protesting even the slightest movement. He recognized the space they were in as the one where he'd doctored the other gunshot patient. "We alone in the room?"

"Yeah. Something's going on out there. And... well, you were shot. Unconscious."

"Did you make the call?"

With a grim expression, she shook her head. "No ELT and the radio didn't work. My guess, he took out the first and disabled the second before he brought us."

"Why didn't he just finish me off?"

She ran a finger through his hair. "Because he knows I won't help him if you die. Now, to that end, what can you tell me about treating your gunshot wound? I followed the instructions in this kit, but I don't know if I did anything right. I should have watched you more closely when you treated the other man, but I...I didn't think it would come to this."

He glanced at the bandaged wound. "Impressive. You stopped the bleeding. I'm good to go for now."

"But does it still hurt?" Her eyes held the telltale shimmer of tears.

"I won't lie to you. It still hurts. But I'm a big boy." Rick reached up and wiped at the corners of her eyes. The one act nearly drained him completely. He had to get his strength back. What were they going to do now? "I have to tell you…" He winced as he shifted and a fire raced through his shoulder. "I have to tell you what happened."

He caught her wrist when she made to move away. "When I was in Afghanistan, my helicopter crashed and burned. I made it out with my copilot. He was unconscious. I tried to get us to safety, but there was just so much chaos around us. The building where I had planned to run for safety blew up. We were taking fire, and there was nothing I could do about it. Every decision I made was the wrong one. I couldn't save him."

"Rick, please, you don't have to tell me."

Rick closed his eyes, remembering the rest, wanting to tell her but knowing it would be too much now.

He felt a sting in his leg—the same burning fire that he felt today in his shoulder—but he kept going. He hefted his unconscious copilot over his shoulder and moved to take cover in the structure of desert bricks. A crumbled building. But it would offer a measure of protection—if he could reach it. Rick was nearly there when he fell to the ground, unable to move. Unable to get completely to safety. He dragged his friend the rest of the way, his legs failing him.

"I wanted, I needed, to save him." The thought of what happened next squeezed his chest. He gulped for air. "Just like I wanted to save you."

The moisture in her eyes surged.

He grabbed her hand and brought it to his lips. "I'm sorry our plan didn't work. You need to find another way to get out. I don't trust Kemp to take you when he goes. See if you can get him to tell you where Aiden is. Then you—"

"Rick," she whispered, tears choking her words. "You're not making any sense. You know that won't work. You're going with me. You have to be the one to get us out. But—" she wiped at her eyes "—I have an idea. I'm going to get that sat phone and use it."

"That's too risky." Rick's words came out garbled even to his own ears, making him realize he was weaker than he'd thought. Maybe he'd lost a little too much blood. With rest, he'd be back to new in no time. The thing was, he didn't know if he would get that here—or ever again.

Rick's eyes shut of their own volition even as he struggled to keep them open. To stay awake. Shay's warm breath tickled his cheek, but he couldn't even produce the smile he felt. Yet he couldn't stop the response in his heart.

I love you, Shay.

Had Rick said the words out loud to her? He wasn't sure. Probably for the best if he hadn't.

He couldn't deny the way his feelings for her had grown, but he still knew she was safer with just about any other good man than with Rick.

SEVENTEEN

Shay stared down at Rick.

Was he asleep? Unconscious? She felt his pulse, measured his breathing and was relieved to hear that both were steady. He needed rest and his body claimed it, but all signs indicated that his condition had stabilized.

The words he'd just said... They wrapped around her, warm and inviting, promising everything her heart longed for. The heat of those three little words came close to melting through the barriers she'd erected to protect herself.

But had she heard him right?

He'd started slurring his words at the end of their conversation, so she couldn't be sure. Even if she'd heard his profession of love correctly, there was a chance he was hallucinating. Things said when a person was injured and delirious didn't count.

She let the tears flow now, even as she hated them for reminding her that she was weak.

She was a woman trying to survive in a man's world—in this case, in a man's gold-mining camp. Tears weren't supposed to come into play. Still, it was better to get the crying over with now. She needed to be tough over the next few hours. She had to be strong enough for the both of them until Rick was back with her in full force.

She sucked in a breath and stood tall, pushing away from the table.

He would be back. She had no doubt of that. *You're coming back to me, Rick Savage.*

"Rick," she whispered. She leaned in and pressed her lips against his, wishing he could hear her. Hoping he didn't. "I love you, too."

She hated the emotions that were torturing her now—knowing she loved him, finally admitting it, but being unable, unwilling, to act on her love. Too risky, too dangerous. Not unlike what Shay was about to do for their survival.

Shay looked at the door, garnering the nerve to walk out there and through the chaos of the camp. The men had returned from getting supplies, their bellies full, but they were angry with Kemp. They were in an uproar, too, about Rick.

Kemp, however, had reined in their ire with something more about the gold. That man had a special gift for controlling people.

She marched out the door and into the camp,

which was alight with activity. She'd been such a familiar sight since working on the backhoe that the men didn't even take notice of her. She was a worker like the rest of them. In some ways, this felt like the Deep Horizon hangar.

One of the men saluted her when she passed. Yep. She was one of the boys now. The mechanic. Not someone who was a flight risk. Maybe they all knew she wasn't going anywhere without Rick. They were right about that—but while she might not leave without Rick, she could still make a call.

Absently, she noticed that an uncanny excitement was rippling through the camp.

A good number of the men had congregated at the scar in the earth, digging with shovels. How had Kemp made them believe...

A shout rang through the group and one of them climbed from the hole, his hands raised as if he'd just completed a touchdown.

Shay eyed the main house, where Kemp had gone with the sat phone after helping her deliver Rick to their makeshift hospital. Kemp hadn't wanted to help her drag Rick back. He'd wanted to leave him for the animals, like the other man. But Shay could be convincing, too. She had used leverage, making the most of the sliver of power she held over the man for now.

If she could just make it to Kemp's quarters.

A few more yards.

She prayed he'd be gone by now. Walking backward, she watched the men dance around. What in the world? Had they really struck a solid chunk of gold? Must have been a sizable nugget, but the way they acted, it was as if they were surprised to find it.

What did she know? Maybe if gold were her sole purpose and she found it, then she'd be dancing for joy. But right now the only thing she wanted was to leave this camp safely, with Rick and Aiden by her side. She'd do anything to make that happen.

Shay planted a smile in place and focused on her mission.

Get.

That.

Sat.

Phone.

She took one more glance to make sure the men were still celebrating and not paying any attention to where she was going.

Uh-oh. The first man out of the hole was running toward her, a smile spread across his face. He held the gold nugget in his hand. He wanted to show her?

Are you kidding me?

Shay didn't know what to do. She could try to turn and ignore him and hope he'd leave her be. But could she remain invisible? Just another one of the men? Or should she congratulate him and hope he'd quickly move on?

Behind her, she could hear him coming up on her fast, so she turned and smiled as if she were joining in the fun. As if it were perfectly normal for her to walk around the camp like this. If the men acted this relaxed in the next few hours, drunk on the wine of finding gold, she and Rick might just find Aiden and drive out of here. Forget the plane.

Yeah, right.

She continued walking backward, hoping he'd simply join her, say what he had to say and then walk away. Instead, he placed his arm around her shoulders and planted a big fat kiss on her lips. Shay cringed, hating the smell of alcohol on his breath.

Stay calm. Don't panic.

She giggled and slipped out of his grasp, teasing and flirting a little even as her insides convulsed.

"This is all because of you, lady. You fixed things up around here. You should get your share, too."

Shay faked a polite laugh and then started walking again, hoping he'd get the message that she was a busy woman. He tugged on her, stopping her. Keeping her from her mission. Fortunately, no one had taken notice of either of them.

His smile held a little too much salacious mischief for her comfort level. "What say I get your share and then we take off? We can go anywhere you want."

Incredulity heaved in her chest, but she blinked and smiled, reining in her emotions. Deep inside, she knew if she even hinted at her feelings for Rick, this man would kill him, believing that would somehow give him a chance.

"Sure. That would be…nice."

Hope flooded his gaze. Was he for real?

Shay examined the nugget he held out, acting as though she were as dazzled by it as he was. "How…how many ounces do you suppose this is? What's it worth?"

She started out only pretending to be interested, but holding something of this weight and value in her hands gave her a funny feeling.

"This, sweet lady, is a nugget. We usually don't find them this big. With gold going for around $1,500 a troy ounce, we're all going to be rich. Kemp agreed to share any profit, once he's paid his debt, with us. There's more down there. There has to be more."

Ah. So that was how Kemp had played them. Slowly and meticulously transferring their loyalty to him.

Shay stared at the man, who remained mesmerized by gold and thought he could buy Shay with it. Just the thought of it squeezed her insides, urging her to finish her mission.

"I have something to do first," she said, bridling her fear. "Get me my fair share of gold and we'll meet up later, okay?"

He nodded and took off running back to the pit.

Shay exhaled. Nausea roiled in her stomach at what she had just done, but she didn't allow herself to dwell on it. She pressed forward to Kemp's house, now mere yards from her. Where did Kemp keep his sat phone when it wasn't with him?

Though she kept an even pace as she walked, confident and silent, hoping to blend in, she had the feeling that men watched her. Eyes followed her. The feeling intensified, driving her nerves tighter and tighter.

The next thing Shay knew, she was practically running to Kemp's house. With a burst of alarm, she remembered that he always kept it locked. What had she been thinking? Panic engulfed her, overwhelming any rational thought. She slammed against the door of the main house and turned the knob.

Locked. Of course. She knew that. How could she have made such a mistake?

She banged on the door. At this moment, with the eyes of the men still burning into her, Kemp would almost be a welcome sight.

He opened it. "What's going on?"

Her legs shaking—she was a much weaker person than she'd thought—Shay fell against him. She wanted to gag but swallowed down the urge. He let her all the way in and shut the door. She used the brief reprieve to think of an excuse for her visit.

"The men, did you know they found gold?" she asked, gulping for air.

Kemp slowly turned his head to look out the window. "We've already found gold."

Shay exhaled a calming breath. "No, I mean a big-size nugget. They say there's more."

He frowned. "That's…that's impossible."

"What do you mean?"

"Stay here," he said, and left her standing there.

In his house.

Shay could hardly believe it. Had all reason gone to the wolves because of the gold? She glanced out the window. Kemp was hiking toward the hole. He'd probably already forgotten about her. He figured she was weak without Rick.

Thank You, thank You, thank You, God. Getting this chance was better than finding gold.

Where had she seen the sat phone? Her eyes scanned the small living room and kitchen as she hurried through. Then she headed to Kemp's office. Her fingers skimmed over every inch of it before she tugged a file drawer open.

There.

Shay's knees grew weak. It couldn't be this easy. Her hands shook violently as she tugged out the case that held the phone. Setting the case on the table, she glanced out the window. She couldn't see Kemp from where she sat, but he was probably dancing with joy, too, after seeing their wealth. He would go ballistic when that one man tried to collect Shay's fair share. Hopefully that would keep him distracted for a while longer, because he would *definitely* go ballistic if he caught her with his phone.

She opened the case and stared down. How did she use this thing? She tugged a quick reference guide from the pocket of the case and scanned the instructions.

Outside? She'd have to go outside to get a signal. Heart racing, Shay swiped her slick palms down her pants. Risky enough to try this in the house, but if she left the cover of these walls, she'd expose herself. Someone would see her.

Unless…she moved to the window and looked out. She didn't think there was a man or guard who wasn't hovering at the pile of dirt and the hole in the earth now. They'd struck gold after all. A real nugget, according to the one man. Kemp had said nuggets of any real size weren't that common, and then he'd acted surprised they'd found something.

His reaction was a little strange.

But Shay didn't care about that right now. She shut the case and tucked it back in the filing cabinet, then crammed the phone and the instructions under her jacket, still stained with Rick's blood. Then Shay went to the room where she'd slept and climbed out the window, ignoring her shaking legs lest she collapse from fear. This was by far the riskiest thing she'd done yet.

But she should have done it long ago. They just hadn't known how things would turn out.

Shay followed the instructions on the sheet, stepping out into open space, away from the trees and building.

After turning on the phone, she moved the antennae and waited to catch a satellite signal, then dialed the country code and Deep Horizon phone number.

Oh, Lord, please let Connor pick up. She didn't know his cell phone number by heart. Behind the building, she had maybe a few minutes before someone discovered her. She'd only have time for one call—and a quick one, at that. If Kemp returned to the house, he'd want to know where she was. He'd realize his mistake in leaving her alone in his house too soon.

A familiar and welcome voice answered.

"Connor? Connor!" Shay drew in a breath to calm herself. To speak clearly. "We're here at a mining camp. We're in trou—"

Kemp's face filled her vision. His hand swiped across her head, knocking her to the ground.

Fire in his shoulder again.

Rick stirred. Reached over and touched the bandage covering the aching wound. He let his arm drop back again and exhaled long and hard. Struggling to his elbow, he got his bearings. He was in the same room where he'd doctored up the other gunshot victim.

He swiped a hand down his face. Where was Shay? Where was anybody, for that matter?

What was the last thing she'd said to him? He scrunched up his eyes, struggling for clarity.

Sat phone. She'd planned to get the sat phone. *Oh, Lord, no.* He'd made the wrong choice by fighting with Kemp. Again. The wrong choice again. Getting injured had left her to take all the risks herself. And that meant that once more someone would get hurt because he was such an idiot.

Not just anyone.

The woman he loved.

Despite the hurt pounding against his ribs, sending pain through his body, Rick pushed to sit. Dizziness swept over him, but it didn't matter. He was better than this. He'd been trained to survive in one of the worst places in the world. This was nothing.

Get it together, Savage.

Inhaling deeply, he stood and pushed beyond the waves of nausea and dizziness. Shay was out there somewhere alone. He had to find her. Rick grabbed the jacket that had been thrown to the floor and saw the bloodied hole where he'd been shot. He tossed it aside and clutched an oversize shirt off a hook on the wall. He slid that on, then snatched a knit cap and put it on, too. That was all the disguise he could manage.

Rick paused at the door and took a peek outside. Darkness had fallen. A couple of men sat around the campfire by the hole where others continued digging. The jig was cranked and running. Floodlights blasted the place. He was surprised to see them continue digging at night. Could they even afford to run those lights?

He took a step outside and instantly he felt it. The upbeat staccato of digging by hand, the laughter and excitement.

Gold.

They'd struck gold. And by the sounds of it, they'd found a lot.

Rick closed the door behind him and jogged down the steps. He fled around the corner, hoping to stay in the cover of darkness and yet look as if he were just another one of the guys about his business. He walked like a man with someplace important to go and glanced into every window of every building he passed.

Ignoring the unending pain. Pressing through the dizziness. He was reliving a scene from his past and this time, he would get the people he cared about to safety.

An ATV rolled up to the mess hall. Rick slinked into the shadows, then crept along the edge of the woods to the kitchen. Maybe Shay was in there. They'd seen the sat phone there with Kemp several times.

"God, please, don't let me mess this up. Please, let me get her out of here. Let her be where I can get her. Let me find Aiden. Please… make a way."

Light flooded out of the window in the back of the kitchen and Rick pressed against the wall, determined to peek through cautiously. Someone might be standing at the sink doing dishes, so he didn't want to be seen. He watched the shadows and light and when he was sure it was safe, he edged closer and looked inside.

Shay!

Kemp suddenly appeared and slapped her

across an already bruised face. She faced off with him, defiant to the last. Defiant in spite of her tears. The woman had fire and guts.

But rage boiled up inside of Rick at the sight of what Kemp was doing to her. All because Rick hadn't been there to protect her. He couldn't just stand here and watch as Kemp grabbed her shoulder and squeezed, hurting her. He gripped the doorknob, ready to burst into the kitchen, but held himself back from entering. Wait…he had to do this right.

God, help me.

He looked through the window again to count the men inside, easily seen in the room's electric light. Not so easy for them to see him outside in the darkness.

Someone entered the mess hall, clomping inside. A voice called for Kemp. One of the two men Rick had seen arriving on the ATV?

Whoever it was, his arrival made Kemp go pale.

He shoved Shay against the counter before turning his attention to someone he feared. Rick saw it in his eyes.

Was this the chance he and Shay needed to get away? Or did the new arrivals herald a disaster that would engulf them with no chance of escape?

EIGHTEEN

Shay clutched the counter, grateful that Kemp had let her go. He'd turned a few shades of pale when someone had ground out his name. Had she seen terror in his eyes?

"So you thought you could outwit us, did you?" The man had a hateful, growling voice.

A familiar voice.

Kemp left the kitchen for the dining hall, but Shay could still see him through the serving window. She kept her head down, wishing she had longer hair to cover her eyes, and watched the scene play out, while her mind scrambled with how to get out of here.

When the man took his hat off, Shay froze. He was one of the men who had tried to kill her and Rick in the truck. Who'd *thought* he'd succeeded in killing her and Rick by shoving their Jeep over the side of a cliff. They'd wanted to keep her and Rick from making the trip to the mining claim, and now she understood why. They feared Kemp was a flight risk if he could get a mechanic to the claim. Or maybe they just didn't want to split the gold with any more people?

Her heart thrummed erratically, turning her breaths into gasps. She was sure the man would hear her and look straight at her.

Kill her right then.

One of the miners stood from the table, the chair scraping the floor in the dead silence. "What's going on, Kemp? Who are these men?"

"None of your concern." Kemp had regained some of his bristle. "Leave us."

Suspicious, the miner narrowed his eyes.

She had to get out of here. Find Rick. She fumbled around with a pan on the stove, pretending to be working in the kitchen, but no one was paying any attention to her. Everyone was too focused on the face-off between Kemp and this new threat.

He'd double-crossed someone else and they were here to collect.

"We want what's owed us. You can have the rest, if there's anything left." They guffawed as if they'd played a real joke on Kemp. And maybe they had.

Shay eyed the back door to the kitchen. How could a few inches seem so far? Easing along the counter, she studied the seasonings on the spice rack, reminding herself to just act normal.

As soon as she was near the door, she drew in a breath, worked up the nerve then quietly slipped out, closing it softly behind her, praying no one had noticed.

She took one step into the shadows and came face to face with a man.

Her mouth opened to scream, but his hand clamped over it. At the same moment, recognition flooded her.

Rick!

Shay almost collapsed with relief, but Rick supported her. He ushered her away from the kitchen and deeper into the shadows, into the woods behind the buildings. A place they could talk without being seen or heard. Shay leaned into him, fearing she might actually crumple as the terror drained from her body.

"Oh, Rick," she choked in a sob against his shirt. All that mattered right now was just that he was here.

"Shh." He wrapped his arms around her, his voice calming. "You're safe."

She'd never thought he could be so tender, but through all of this, he'd shown her that and much more. Was it any wonder she'd fallen in love with him?

"It's okay," he said, and released her to look in her eyes. "We have to get out of here. Quick. Tell me what happened. What's going on?"

"Okay, well…" She started to shake and hated herself for it. "They found gold. A lot of it. And then just now in the kitchen, those two men who ran us off the cliff showed up wanting to collect what Kemp owes them."

Rick frowned. "What about the sat phone? I specifically told you not to go look for it. So did you?"

"Yes… I…" Shay nodded. "I found it and made the call but didn't get to finish it."

Gripping her shoulders, Rick drew her closer. "Is help coming?"

"It should be. I told Connor we were in trouble. I didn't get it all out, but he knows we're at the mine. He has Reg, his FBI brother, working security detail and he has connections, doesn't he?"

"Yes. You did good." Rick gently touched the bruise around her eye. "Did Kemp do this to you?"

"It doesn't matter now. Let's go."

Rick pulled his hand away. "Aiden. I have to find him. Then we'll head for the airplane. If that doesn't work, we'll wait these guys out in the wilderness until Connor sends help for us."

"I agree we should find him if we can. But, Rick, be careful. Those men in there. I think they're going to kill Kemp and then everyone else. They didn't say it in so many words, but they're not going to get the gold without a battle."

Machine-gun fire rattled off in the distance.

Rick tensed, a faraway look sweeping over his features. "Let's go."

He tugged Shay behind him along the edge of the woods, listening as commotion and fury spread through the camp.

Men scrambled from the dig and picked up their arms, understanding all too well that someone had come to take their gold. Pushing through the edges of the camp, Rick stopped at a boulder and turned to Shay.

He held her face in his hands. "I need you to stay here. I'm going to find Aiden. I'll come back for you."

"Wait. Rick, are you crazy? No. You can't." Shay couldn't wait for him here, not knowing if he'd return. Not knowing what was happening.

"Shay, this is a war zone now. You know how to fix your planes. This is what I know how to do. Trust me, okay? It's easier for me to find him if I go on my own. No one is going to see you or look for you out here. Just duck down in the shadows of this rock. Don't worry. I'm not going far."

Rick angled his head, looking at her lips. Then he kissed her hard and quick.

The next thing Shay knew, he'd disappeared, leaving her there stunned from his kiss and hiding behind a rock.

The bomb went off in Rick's mind.

He felt the concussion of air again, his past propelling him, tossing him forward as he bolted for the building.

This was Afghanistan all over again. His mission all over again. And once again, he knew that people would die.

But last time, there wasn't a woman he loved waiting in the shadows for him to return. Waiting for him to take her to safety. This time, he'd have to get it right—he wouldn't accept any other option.

The rapid-fire shots of an automatic weapon belted out, resounding throughout the camp. They drowned out all other sounds except Rick's long, hard breaths, gasps for air as he shoved away the flashbacks.

Shay was counting on him.

Keeping to the shadows, he crept to one of the buildings, hoping to find a clue to his brother's location.

The shadow of a man carrying a rifle drew long in front of the building, approaching Rick's position. His cadence and posture were familiar, and after a minute of thinking, Rick remembered the guy—he'd been the one to shoot the four-point buck.

Rick pressed against the wall.

Wait for it.

The man hesitated at the corner, but Rick had the advantage of seeing his shadow. The man could see nothing of Rick. Didn't even know he was there.

Rick had to be quick. Catch the man before he whipped his weapon around.

Sensing someone waiting, the rifleman aimed his weapon into the darkness. But Rick reached out and knocked the rifle down, then drove the butt of the weapon up into the man's jaw, disarming him in one fell swoop.

While adrenaline coursed through his body he no longer felt the pain of his gunshot wound. Rick squeezed the man's throat as he pressed him against the building. "Where's my brother?"

The man struggled to speak. "I…don't.. know…"

Rick punched him in the gut. "I don't have time for this. Where would Kemp keep someone hidden?"

The rifleman shook his head, the whites of his eyes showing his fear, stirring up far too many memories of past battlefields.

Focus. He had to focus. "This is your last chance," Rick warned.

"Kemp held someone up in the old mining shaft. Told us to leave him alone."

"Mining shaft?" Realization rocked him—why hadn't he thought of that? Of course! This had been a hard-rock mine before it had turned placer—there were plenty of shafts sitting empty.

"Where is it?"

Rifleman motioned with his head. "Just southeast of the camp."

"You'd better not be lying, or I'll find you."

The guy nodded, pleading with his eyes for mercy. "You're not going to kill me?"

Now, if he'd really thought that Rick would kill him anyway, why had he given up the information? He didn't bother to answer, just slammed the butt of the weapon against the rifleman's head again, this time knocking him unconscious. Didn't need anyone giving away their plans. The man might actually survive the war zone if he stayed unconscious, away from the fray.

Rick turned his attention to the building to his right, which kept him in the shadows. The same building where Rick had treated the wounded man. Where Rick himself had been taken for Shay to treat his own wound.

He made his way inside and grabbed as much ammo as he could, along with a couple of extra coats someone had left behind. Aiden and Shay would need them. He slipped one on, then slung the other two over his shoulder. After peering through the window, he crept out and into the shadows again.

Armed and in his element, Rick maneuvered back to Shay under cover of darkness. He had no idea who was winning the fight behind him but it wasn't his battle. His only thought was to get Shay and Aiden to safety.

The floodlights zapped, sparked and finally popped out completely, leaving the night bathed in darkness. For a moment, he couldn't see, which was good because that meant no one else could see, either. But his eyes quickly adjusted and the moonlight was enough to illuminate the few yards between the building where he remained pressed against the wall and the place where he'd left Shay.

A feeling of anxiety crawled over him, leaving him unhappily certain that Shay was no longer beside the rock where he'd left her. Where he'd *told* her to stay so he could find her. From the shadows, he crept low to the ground until he made the cover of the trees. With stealth, he edged closer to the rock and froze. He'd been right to worry—she wasn't there.

He listened for night sounds, but animal life and insects had gone silent in the wake of gunfire. The men were still positioning themselves, the rattle of automatic weapons spraying with abandon every few seconds.

All else was quiet around him. He bent down and found a pebble, then tossed it. He heard the small rock hit the ground a few yards away and hoped he would hear Shay react.

Nothing.

Disappointment and alarm twisted inside. Had she left willingly, disregarding his request that she remain here? No. She'd understood how important it was to remain hidden where Rick could find her. But he didn't like to think of the other possible reason she was gone. He'd only been a few yards away from her. How could this happen?

Gruff and threatening, a man's voice drifted on the breeze from somewhere deeper in the woods. Weapon at the ready, Rick felt as if he were in the war zone again, wearing his fatigues, creeping between the buildings of the small Afghan village. He'd been a marine helicopter pilot but had plenty of experience in ground operations, as well.

His eyes adjusting to the darkness, he inched forward, searching for the man. And for Shay.

A rustling of leaves up ahead drew Rick's attention. Looking through the scope, Rick stole silently through the woods. *Where are you, Shay? Show yourself.*

Then he saw the half-drunk hulking form leaning against a tree. Rick fingered the trigger guard. Had he been the one to chase Shay off? If so, where was she now? Rick remained still, listening to every sound, waiting for any movement.

From behind a tree, Shay's form came into a sliver of moonlight breaking through the thick forest. A rock in her hand, she tiptoed toward the man.

Rick considered his options. He couldn't let Shay try to take him down with the rock. But if Rick gave his position away and it turned out the man had a weapon, he might not be fast enough to keep the man from turning the gun on him, or on Shay. Indecision squeezed his gut. Sweat trickled down his back.

But even as Rick was frozen in place, Shay made her move, and when she lifted the rock, the man turned, revealing the gun in his hand.

NINETEEN

Shay held the rock up—she had no choice but to strike.

Not to kill him. Her intention was to knock him senseless so she could get away. She'd hoped he'd be easy to attack. He was so drunk that he hadn't even noticed when she'd slipped away from his side to find a rock to use.

When he'd come to collect her as she'd agreed, she'd pretended to play along, hoping for a chance to get away—or get rescued.

Rick, where are you?

She knew where he was—he was in the camp, trying to find Aiden. Shay was on her own now.

Moonbeams swept across the grizzly miner's sluggish features as he turned toward her. At the sight of her hand clutching the rock, his eyes widened.

Then he aimed a gun at her face.

Shay felt her heart stop. Felt her own eyes widen. She wasn't faster than a bullet and hesitated for a millisecond too long. A shot rang out, and Shay's knees buckled from fear.

But it was the man in front of her who fell the hardest, toppling forward into Shay, who scrambled back in the dirt just in time to avoid falling under his dead weight.

Rick appeared out of nowhere and helped her to her feet. She'd never been so glad to see him.

"*You* shot him?"

He nodded and pressed a finger against the man's neck, looking for a pulse. "He's dead."

Rick had killed a man. Right in front of her. Just as her mother had been killed. By all logic, she should be feeling terrified of him right now. But...he'd done it to save her life. Knowing that, she couldn't feel afraid of him anymore. Did that mean she was finally ready to let herself love him? Shay's throat grew thick, felt as if it was closing off.

Breathe.... She had to breathe....

Her mind grappling with the truth, Shay sucked in the chilled and moist forest air. Rick forced her to look at him. "Are you hurt?"

Shay shook her head, but she didn't feel all right. Rick peeled the man's fingers from the weapon and examined it. "What do you know?" He gazed at her with eyes full of surprise. "Recognize this?"

"It's yours." She studied the all-too-familiar

weapon with the custom grip. "That makes sense. People just keep aiming that thing at my head."

Rick put it away. "Wait here."

"Rick, no…." she said. He'd left her once before. She wasn't going to let him do that again.

"It's okay, Shay. I'm just heading for the trees right there where I dropped something I brought for you."

Shay waited patiently and Rick returned with a coat.

"Here, put this on." He handed her the too-large parka. "We have to get out of here."

Slipping into the coat meant for a man, Shay smiled as she looked down at the proof that Rick had been thinking about her when he was in the middle of the gunfire back at the camp.

Trudging ahead, he clearly expected Shay to follow. He seemed agitated. Or maybe he was just focused, in the zone.

She looked back at the dead man. "But what about—?"

"Leave him for now. If we don't get far away before the war is over back there, they'll look for us, find us and then we'll join him."

That reasoning was good enough for Shay. She stayed close behind Rick, who maneuvered through the woods with the ease of the soldiers she'd seen in movies. "What about Aiden?"

"I found out where he is, I hope. That's where we're headed now." Rick paused and waited, holding his hand up.

Shay instinctively realized he meant for her to stop. Stop walking. Stop talking.

Ten seconds ticked by. Fifteen. Twenty.

The woods were quiet around them. Too quiet. Shay's legs cramped. She needed to move. But Rick was as still as a tree, unmoving, blending into his surroundings. She'd have to follow his lead.

A gust of arctic air whipped over her, reminding her of the impending storm. She glanced up at what she could see of the sky through the trees. Clouds were moving in. They'd soon cover the moon.

Then it would be black out here.

Finally, Rick angled his own head at her and lifted a finger to his lips. He wanted her to maintain the silence…but it was time to start moving again.

He crept forward, and Shay followed as quietly as she could. Rick shoved through the undergrowth, pushing deeper into the woods, farther from the camp.

Shouts and gunfire grew distant. How long would the shoot-out last? Would anyone survive? The thought of all the possible death sickened Shay, made her dizzy and weak. She imagined this wasn't what Kemp's grandfather had had in mind when he'd bequeathed the claim to his grandson.

She touched Rick's arm, just needing to feel connected to him. He was in his element now, protecting her, but somehow he seemed distant. She didn't like it.

"What now?" she asked, her question soft like the first snowfall.

"See that?"

Shay squinted, trying to focus through the darkness. His eyes must be much better than hers. He wasn't even peering through the scope and he could see it.

"The opening to a mine shaft," he whispered. "Aiden's supposed to be in there."

Rick moved toward the opening, and Shay followed closely. She couldn't see a thing in the shadows and couldn't help but be impressed by how confidently Rick moved even in the darkness.

Shay had known Rick was an amazing pilot, but she'd never seen this side to him. Never had cause to see him in action as a marine, and it left her dazed. He was like a large predatory cat, prowling, invisible in the night. Her heart pounded at the sight of him. How she admired everything about this man.

At the opening of the shaft, Rick waited and listened. The cavity didn't offer any signs of life.

"I don't like this. Something's wrong." Rick looked at Shay. "I'm going in. You stay here."

"Look what happened last time you left me behind. Someone found me."

"It's completely dark in there. Dangerous, too. It could drop off into nothingness. The ground is most likely unstable. This could be a dead end as far as Aiden is concerned."

"I don't care. I'll be right behind you."

Rick nodded and stepped into the old, dank mining shaft. Planting her hand against the cold, moist stone, she trailed him into the mine. She hadn't realized just how completely dark it would be. She couldn't see her hand in front of her face, nor could she hear Rick's breathing near her or the crunching of his boots in the dirt—but then, he knew how to be quiet.

That was unfortunate for her. Maybe she couldn't follow him after all.

She reached out to touch him but her hand grasped empty air. Something told her not to speak his name. Not to give them away.

Rick inched forward in the shaft, acutely focused and alert to his surroundings.

He ignored the signals his own body was sending—the pain in his shoulder, the weakness that washed over him in waves. Those could be dealt with once he'd gotten them all away from here.

Sensing that Shay was no longer close behind, he glanced back and saw that she'd remained near the opening—he could just see her silhouette. Best to leave her there until he'd ferreted out whatever threat waited for them.

His gut churned with images of finding Aiden dead. Another loved one whom Rick had let down. If that turned out to be the case, he didn't know how he would live with himself.

If Aiden was in here, alive and well, he must be deep inside, because there wasn't any evidence of someone imprisoned inside the shaft so far. Darkness grew thicker and tendrils of uncertainty slithered through his mind, making him feel as if he was on an impossible mission.

In the end, he might call out Aiden's name, but right now he had a feeling silence was his best option.

When the opening of the shaft disappeared, Shay along with it, Rick reached out and touched the wall. The shaft wasn't by any means hot, though beads of sweat spread over him from his nerves and the pain he was in. Salty moisture dripped into his eyes. He ignored it as he followed the shaft as it made a turn, angling to the right.

Rick steadied his breathing, but unfortunately, the slightest exhale resounded through the man-made cavern. Tingles rolled over his arms. He held his breath. Someone was in here with him.

Right.

Next.

To him.

Such an eerie feeling—that sixth sense that told you when you weren't alone. That maybe someone was watching you. In this case, he wasn't being watched. Too dark for that.

But he was being…anticipated. Expected?

Attacked!

In an instant, a light flashed on. A log rammed into the side of Rick's head. He struggled to maintain his footing and his consciousness.

Then the man was on him, trying to wrestle the rifle away from him. Keeping his grip on the weapon, Rick held off the man while grappling for the handgun in his pocket.

Realization dawned as he found he recognized the shape of the body in front of him and the way that the man moved. In the dim light of the flashlight that had fallen to the ground, he even came to recognize the face fighting him.

"Aiden!"

In his surprise, Rick let down his guard and Aiden wrestled the rifle from his grasp. He aimed it at Rick, his finger on the trigger guard.

"Aiden. What are you doing? It's me!"

Aiden blinked, then cocked his head. "Rick?"

"Yes. It's me." Relief rushed through Rick so fast he fell against the rock wall, pebbles sliding past him. "You can put down that rifle now."

Wariness battling across his features, his brother lowered the weapon. Rick pushed away from the wall and grabbed his brother in a bear hug.

"You're alive." Squeezing his eyes shut, he concentrated on taking in his brother's sturdy, living, breathing body. *I can't believe you're alive.*

He'd tried to prepare himself for the worst. Tried. But failed miserably. That was one thing he didn't mind failing at.

When Rick released Aiden, he looked him over. "So what happened? I thought you were being kept prisoner here."

When he lifted his hands, Rick saw his raw wrists. "I spent hours digging away at the dirt and rock where the chains were secured into the wall," Aiden explained. "Just back there a ways, someone built a shelter. The wooden planks, everything is pretty intact, because it was kept away from the elements all these years. I found a tool that I used to work the locks off. It was time-consuming. And I had to time it just right. My plan was to be free so I could take Kemp down before he came back. I couldn't let him catch me midescape."

"So why are you still here?"

"I was headed out when I saw someone coming. I heard gunfire, a lot of gunfire. I wanted to get my hands on Kemp and his gun before I went to rescue you and Shay—"

Aiden jerked his head toward the shaft opening. "Where is she? Did you get her out, too?"

"She's at the entrance. We should—"

Shay stepped into the light from the flashlight, which was quickly beginning to fade.

"Aiden." She sighed his name. "You're alive."

She rushed to him and hugged him, too. Aiden stepped away from her and swiped a hand through his hair. "I must look and smell awful."

"Nothing new there," Rick said, teasing. He was so glad to have Aiden alive. Glad they were together.

"Sorry for clobbering you over the head," Aiden said. "I thought you were Kemp. I was going to take his gun and come for you. Didn't mean to point the rifle at you. Had plans to rescue you, but I see you've managed to find your own way."

Rick remembered the look in Aiden's eyes when he'd aimed the rifle. The look of a man intent on harm. A man who was angry and dazed. In another world. It had taken him seconds to recognize Rick. And in those seconds, he might have shot and killed his brother.

Had that been how Shay had felt when Rick had done the same thing to her? His gut churned. How could she ever forgive him for something like that—much less consider a relationship with him? Clearly, he was no good for her.

He took a couple of steps away from her. Just to be clear to himself.

"Barely," he said, shoving the anxiety of his feelings for Shay away for now. "This isn't over yet. We still need to make it to the airplane and get out of here before they stop fighting each other and figure out that we've escaped. If Kemp is still alive, he'll probably head straight for the airplane as soon as he gets the chance, if he hasn't already."

Shay tugged a wire from her pocket. "He might go to the plane, but he won't get very far without this. It's a wire from the ignition system."

"That doesn't mean he won't try," Rick said. "In fact, he might even try to find you so you can fix it."

"I don't think he'll survive the slaughter." Aiden coughed. "So how did they find out anyway?"

"Find out?"

"You know, about the gold."

Rick stared. He wasn't following.

"Rick, there is no gold. Kemp fooled them into digging the mine just to stall them until he could get the Cessna fixed and get out."

"What are you talking about? Of course there's gold."

Aiden ran both hands through his hair. "No, there isn't, and he knows it. That's the reason he kept me locked up in here. Kept me away from everyone. I was the only one who knew the truth. I found the letter in the airplane that detailed the geology of his claims. This site was a long shot. This isn't the place that his grandfather struck anything worth digging."

Sagging against the dank rock wall, Rick blew out a breath. "He's been scamming us all. Not that I wanted the gold, but the thing is—"

"They found gold," Shay said. "I saw one of the nuggets. It didn't look like much to me, but the men, the atmosphere in the camp, everything changed after that."

"What if Kemp just planted it?" Risk asked. "You know, to keep them going."

Shay slowly shook her head. "I was the one to tell him they'd found gold and he looked stunned. In fact, now his reaction makes more sense."

She wrapped her arms around herself. "After finding the nugget worthy to celebrate, that's when the two who ran us off the road showed up to collect on their debt," Shay said. "They've been keeping tabs on the progress. Maybe that's why they wanted us dead—because they knew Kemp was just playing them and would run the second he had a chance…using that Cessna. To keep him from getting away, they couldn't let me fix the plane. But how'd they know that gold had finally been found?"

"Someone from the camp had to be keeping them informed," Rick said.

"Could be. Maybe the rifleman—he left the camp a lot to hunt. Maybe he had a satellite phone of his own that he used once he got away from camp."

"I can't believe I've been locked up here the whole time because there was no gold, and in the end there was."

"Yeah, you don't know what you were missing facing off with a bunch of gun-toting maniacs every day." Rick's tone was a little sarcastic but seasoned with humor. He picked up the rifle. "Before we go, let's pray."

Aiden's expression grew somber and he nodded. His faith in God had been tenuous at best, but Rick believed in his brother. Believed he would find his way to overcome. Rick offered up heartfelt words requesting protection and a way out. And he thanked God for leading him to his brother.

Their prayers finished, quiet filled the old mine shaft. Rick shifted to ease the pain in his shoulder, dreading what was ahead of them. "Let's move out."

The words took his mind back to places he didn't want to go.

"The airstrip is on the far side of the camp, opposite this shaft," Shay said. "How do we get there without getting caught again?"

"We need to get there quickly but without risking our lives. We'll move as fast as we can but we'll need to stay as far away from the claim as possible without veering too far off course. We want to approach the airstrip from the other side without Kemp or anyone else spotting us. It's going to be tricky."

They had to beat Kemp to the plane, get it running and make it out before the snowstorm buried them.

We could already be too late.

TWENTY

Rick slid the handgun over to Aiden, but he kept a firm grip on the rifle.

"Lock and load," he said as they exited the shaft.

Shay witnessed the look they shared. Two brothers who knew the score. Two ex-marines who knew how to handle this operation. If anyone could make this happen, these two could. As the temperature dipped, an unrelated chill shivered over her. She was not at all eager to leave the shelter of the mine shaft and trek through the woods. They'd grown even darker as the predicted storm moved in and covered the moon and stars, blocking out their only light.

Although Shay knew her way around an airplane in the dark and was certain she could get the plane running, the weather worried her as much as Kemp and his men. With no radio and nothing but the instruments, how would they

fly out if the weather was bad? In zero visibility, they were going nowhere.

The task seemed impossible. But that was the
only choice they'd been given. They couldn't
count on help sweeping in to save them. Any law
enforcement that might be on its way after her
call to Connor would take time to get here, and
the storm would slow a possible rescue down, if
not halt their efforts completely. Then it would
be too late for Rick, Shay and Aiden.

They were on their own.

Rick led the way down the path, followed by
Shay with Aiden last.

Shivering with the drop in temperature, Shay
would be grateful when they made it to the
plane—it could at least serve as shelter. Honestly, she'd be grateful when they made it out
of Alaska, period. Thankfully the exertion of
hiking through the woods generated warmth.

If they survived the night, flying out in the
morning would take away their one advantage—
darkness. Any way you looked at it, they had
to hurry. She also needed to rewire the ignition
so they could be ready to go as soon as conditions allowed.

The two strong men with her made her feel
safe. She still hadn't forgotten the memory of
that day in the office when Rick had aimed his
gun at her. For a long time, Shay had thought she

could never get past that, at least on a more personal level. In that moment when the drunken miner had aimed, ready to fire, Rick had saved her. He'd *killed* to save her.

Hiking in front of her, he turned his head to the side, making sure she was behind him, and Aiden, too. Seeing him in action like this, she tried to imagine living through what he'd lived through. She recalled what he'd told her of his time as a marine helicopter pilot—the crash that stayed with him in his dreams.

She doubted she could ever fully grasp what he'd gone through, but she saw things clearly now. Rick had opened up to her, showing the deepest part of who he was at his core, so that she could trust him. And with that trust, that understanding of who Rick was, Shay could finally remove the restraints on the love she had for him—a love that felt as though it would explode if she didn't open that bottle cap.

She hoped she would get the chance to tell him.

Except she wasn't sure he wanted to know. Back at the mine shaft, he'd pulled away from her. Physically…and emotionally. She'd felt it, but she didn't know why.

As if reflecting her thoughts, the sky took on the dark gray of morning clouds heavy with snow. She hadn't realized just how late it was or how close they were to morning.

At least the storm hadn't started during the night. The clearing that indicated the airstrip became visible through the trees, and Rick slowed up. He brought the rifle to his shoulder and peered through the scope.

Aiden pressed in behind Shay. "What is it?"

"Just checking it out. Making sure no one is waiting for us to step out into the open where they can gun us down."

"Right," Aiden said. "If Kemp is still alive, and he's free from his pursuers, he'll expect us to take the plane."

"What do you think is going on back at the claim?" she asked. Had they all killed each other? Or had Kemp survived the innumerable murderous men he owed money?

Shay hadn't heard any gunfire in a while, but that meant nothing.

"Maybe they're all dead, but we can't know." Aiden stepped forward to stand beside Rick. They waited and listened. "I think we should stay hidden but walk the perimeter just to be sure."

"Roger that," Rick said, and offered a half grin.

Shay couldn't help but smile, too, at how clearly happy Rick was to have Aiden back.

Rick and Aiden led the way together around the perimeter with Shay trailing behind them. They peered through the foliage as they went, moving slowly to avoid notice. After they'd made it three-quarters of the distance around the airstrip, Rick finally stopped.

"The hangar is exactly opposite where the trail opens up on the other side," he said.

She'd noticed that before but she'd had too much other stress going on to think about it. "Why would that be? Seems kind of strange," she said.

"They probably thought they were going to start mining on this side. Who knows? But if anyone bent on finding us or taking the plane hikes up the trail, they'll likely come from that direction and quickly spot us."

"But we'll see them, too," Shay said.

"Right. We're going to move on that plane like we're expecting someone to try to take it from under us." Rick held her gaze. "You ready to fix her up, Shay?"

Panic rose in her chest. "Sure, but don't you need to go through the preflight checklist, too?"

"Aiden will do that while you work. I'll stand guard." Rick looked at her.

"How can we fly in this weather? And without a radio? It isn't safe, is it?"

A grin cracked Aiden's face. "Flying in the

Alaskan bush is different than how we do it in the mainland. No air-traffic control out here, so the lack of a radio doesn't make as much of a difference. I'll fly low, just under the clouds. As long as I can see, I'm good to get us somewhere safe," Aiden said. "I spotted an airstrip halfway between here and Fairbanks on the way in. We should be fine since we don't have to stay in the air that long. We can call for help from there."

"You're safe with Aiden," Rick said. "There's not a better pilot, especially in this kind of weather."

Shay nodded her consent.

"Are we ready to do this thing?" Rick asked.

Aiden gestured for Rick to lead the way.

Rick sucked in a breath as if he were preparing for a serious military operation. "Double time."

Shay understood Rick's marine speak to mean "make it quick." She tucked her head in, parka hood in place, and jammed her hands in her pockets to get them warmed up for the mission ahead. She prepared her thoughts, running through her head what she needed to do to complete the task. Though under normal circumstances, she could do it in her sleep, the pressure and the time constraints were great and she feared her panic might render her useless.

Rick crept in front of her, Aiden behind, the

wo men scanning the perimeter, their weapons
·eady, guarding her as if she were someone im-
)ortant. They rushed across the short distance
o the rudimentary hangar shed.

Reaching the cover of the structure, Shay
·ushed around the Cessna to put the wire back
nto place, connecting the magneto with the ignition starter. She rubbed her hands together and
got busy on the remaining maintenance. Aiden
worked through the flight checklist at the same
ime to make sure they weren't about to fly away
n a death trap. And Rick positioned himself
nearby, peering through the scope of the rifle,
adjusting it so it didn't press against his wound.
The weapon looked as if it were made for him.
She'd just finished her last repair when Rick
spoke.

"Shay?" Tension threaded his voice. "You
done yet?"

She swiped her hands down her pants. "That
should do it."

"Aiden, time to get Shay out of here." Rick
ook aim. "Someone's coming up the trail. I'll
stay behind to give you a chance to get away."

"What?" Aiden's question came out at the
same time as Shay's gasp.

"Rick, get in the plane," Shay pleaded. "We're
all leaving together."

"Aiden, do as I ask."

Aiden stared at Rick long and hard, knowing what leaving Rick behind might mean. Finally he handed over the gun. "You might need this."

"No...." Shay whispered.

"Thanks." Rick took the weapon from his brother, wrapping his hand around the custom grip he'd installed. Strange to think that the gun had traveled all these miles with him and landed in so many different hands. In the end, he had a feeling it would save his life. Regardless, he was glad to have his own weapon to carry home with him if he made it out alive.

"Come on, Shay, we have to go," Aiden said and squeezed her arm. "Rick knows what he's doing."

"Rick thinks he needs to be a hero. But he's already a hero. He doesn't have to do this. Rick..." Shay's voice echoed through him, splitting his heart.

Rick heard Shay fighting Aiden off. Knew the instant she stood next to him.

The engine thrummed to life behind him. Now to convince Shay to leave without him. She gripped his arm, yanking his gaze away from the trail.

"What are you doing? Get on the plane with me, Rick." Anger infused the tears in her eyes.

"Whoever is coming up the trail will shoot

at the plane hoping to render it inoperative. They'll shoot to kill if I don't stay behind and prevent that from happening. One of us has to stay. Aiden is the best man to get the Cessna out of here. I'm better with the rifle."

"You don't have to do this," she said. "I understand that you somehow think you can change the past in Afghanistan with your actions today. But you don't need to sacrifice yourself to make things right. I won't let you. I'm not leaving you."

Rick gripped her arms and pulled her close. How he loved this woman. And that was exactly why he had to do this. But he couldn't tell her that. Couldn't show her that. Not if he wanted to keep her safe. "Forget about me. I'm not the man you think I am."

The wind picked up, gusting all around them, and snow began to fall. It would be a tricky take-off even now—and if they waited any longer, it couldn't happen at all.

"You're wrong. I know exactly who you are and I wouldn't change a thing about you. I love you, Rick Savage."

"If you love me, then let me protect you. I can't let something happen to you. Don't you understand that?" He drove the words home over the wind. "I need you to take the only chance you have and trust me to find my own way out."

He'd said those same words to her before when they'd discussed leaving Aiden. He'd wanted to prepare her then, knowing it might come to this. Tears streamed down her red, frozen cheeks as she nodded. Rick thought his heart would break. This woman saw him for what he was— the whole ugly truth—and she still loved him.

Why, God? Why had he made it to this point only to have to give it up?

Maybe…maybe things could work out if they could survive. "Then go, be safe. I can manage better on my own. Do you understand?"

"Come back to me, Rick." She stood on her toes and planted a sweet and tender kiss against his lips.

"Go with Aiden now. I'll hide in the woods, keep them from shooting you out of the sky."

Shay nodded and stepped away from Rick. She paused just before she climbed into the plane and glanced back at Rick.

"Goodbye, Shay," he said.

She frowned and climbed into the waiting plane, the propellers roaring and ready. *Get her out of here, Aiden.*

The Cessna crept from the hangar and onto the airstrip, then roared forward without wasting a second.

Rick backed into the space where the airplane had been seconds before and watched the trail

He planned to do just as he'd told Shay—protect them from would-be shooters until they were well out of range. His opportunity to live up to his responsibility came just seconds later.

Kemp burst onto the airstrip waving a gun in one hand, a bag thrown over his other shoulder. "Don't leave without me!"

Kemp would have to wait for the authorities with Rick. Unquestionably, the man was up for the task—he'd already proved he was resilient. Rick stepped from the hangar so Kemp would see him and aimed the rifle at him.

"Stop right there, Kemp," he yelled over the deteriorating weather, "or I'll shoot."

"What are you doing? We have to get out of here now." A desperate man, Kemp ran down the airstrip toward the plane as if he could catch it. As if he hadn't heard what Rick had said or seen his intention.

Rick wouldn't shoot him unless he became an imminent threat. Right now he was just a madman chasing a plane. But then Kemp aimed his gun at the Cessna.

"Kemp!" Rick yelled, giving him one more chance. "I'll shoot you if you don't put down the gun."

Kemp took aim and Rick fired, too, but the rifle misfired and jammed, and Kemp got a shot off at the Cessna, which hadn't gotten out of range yet.

Come on, Aiden. God, please keep them safe.

The rifle's misfire didn't go unnoticed by Kemp, and the man ran toward Rick. Behind Kemp, several men who had also heard the shots started from the woods and across the airstrip.

Oh, man.

With the men on him now, he didn't have time to clear the jam only to discover he couldn't fire the rifle. Without the rifle, Rick didn't have enough ammo to take on all those men. Nor could he hope to be much of a threat with just his 9 mm handgun, but he cocked it anyway, took aim and fired again at the snow near Kemp's running feet, hoping to deter him. Then Rick disappeared behind the wall of the hangar and ran for cover. He exited on the other side and slipped into the protection of the woods so he could fire at anyone who took aim at the Cessna.

The airplane was in the air now, and he watched it make a wide, circling sweep. A measure of relief swept through him that Aiden and Shay could make it to safety. His brother was a top-notch pilot, experienced in flying under the worst conditions. She was in good hands.

As for himself… Rick was in God's hands now. There was little left for him to do other

han pray for help to arrive soon. If those men
lidn't kill him first, the weather would come in
a close second.

TWENTY-ONE

Shay pressed her hands against her eye sockets, trying to keep the moisture and the pain inside.

When Rick had said goodbye, she'd had a feeling he'd meant it for good. She could see it in his eyes.

Aiden circled the airstrip at a safe distance.

"This is wrong. All wrong," she said, watching what was happening below. "How could you leave him, Aiden?"

"You think I like being forced into leaving him behind? Those men would take us out before we made the runway if it weren't for Rick. There wasn't any other way, Shay."

A sob lodged in her throat. "We have to help him."

"Right now I need to concentrate on flying. Getting us to safety before there's zero visibility. If we'd had any other choice, I would have taken it, but remember, Rick is trained to survive. He's probably better off than Kemp or any of his men. He'll come out of this, don't worry."

"How can you be so sure?"

"It's more than a matter of skills. You've given him something to live for, Shay. I can see it when he looks at you."

"But the way he said goodbye, I don't think he's planning to make it out alive."

Aiden frowned and Shay wasn't sure if he was frowning in concentration as snow beat the small plane or if he had a bad feeling about Rick, too.

"Let's go back," she said.

The engine stammered. Shay's heart clenched as she realized what that meant. "There must have been water in the system. And it's freezing now, blocking the fuel flow."

Kemp hadn't been careful with the fuel he'd used.

"There's an airstrip up a ways where we can get help," Aiden said. "But I don't know if we can make that distance."

Shay gripped the seat, her knuckles white. Had she survived Kemp and his men only to die in a plane crash?

Rick pushed deeper into the woods, the snow beginning to pile up even beneath the forest canopy. Each step drained his energy. He paused, listening to the distant hum of the Cessna, hoping the sound would drift from range soon. Only it wasn't the sound of a vibrant and healthy plane he heard. The engine stuttered and so did Rick's heart.

She's icing up.

God, please, no. He sank to his knees and prayed.

"Haven't we been through enough, God? Please, don't let me have sent them to their death." His heart palpitated as he waited, listening, not caring that Kemp and others were most likely headed this way.

The Cessna steadied out in the distance. Rick sent up a heartfelt thanks and shoved to his feet, pushing forward in the driving snow. Even in the snow, Aiden had decent visibility if the clouds were above a few thousand feet. He could get them to safety as long as the small plane didn't have a heart attack and die on them. And even if it did, Aiden could bring her in for a landing in the snow.

They could survive. They *had* to survive. That thought was all that kept Rick going. Twigs snapped somewhere in the forest behind him and he pushed harder.

Farther.

Deeper.

Kemp would have to be crazy to follow him

out in this storm, but at this point, Kemp was a man with few options, same as Rick.

Rick trudged in a wide circle heading back to the mine shaft. Despite the danger from the men, he couldn't ignore the presence of a known shelter in the face of the coming storm. And anyway, the more distance he put between himself and the camp, the more difficult time a search-and-rescue team would have in finding him.

Rick found himself in front of a deep gorge. He'd edge the gorge for a while until he could double back to the mine shaft. At this point, he'd rather suffer through a fistfight, dodge bullets, whatever it took, than slowly freeze to death in the Alaskan wilderness. He had to get warm, and soon.

He didn't know how long it would take for Connor to send assistance, but he knew the man well enough to know that he could call in favors if that was what it took to get help in spite of the weather.

With that thought, hope infused Rick, warming his insides. His hiking picked up and he breathed easier. All he had to do was last a little longer.

But then Kemp stepped from the forest, aiming his weapon directly at Rick.

The flame of hope Rick had felt moments ago

stuttered as the Cessna had. Kemp had found him, and the others would, too.

Kemp was between him and the cover of the forest. Rick stood motionless. Kemp struggled to get his breath, then finally dropped a bag at his feet.

"You're going to get me out of this. That was the deal."

"I don't recall agreeing to a deal like that. Besides, any deals made were under duress."

"Your brother and your girl got out. If I didn't need you to get me out, I'd kill you right here."

Rick wasn't sure what the guy expected from him. "There's nothing I can do about the weather."

"You know how to survive. And you can keep those hounds off me."

Taking a step forward, Rick eyed the bag on the ground. "Why are they still chasing you? After all, they found gold. No. Wait. Let me guess. You took the gold."

"It's not what you think. I need it to pay what I owe to my debtors, not to those snarling miscreants who shot up my camp and tried to kill you. They have nothing to do with me. My grandfather promised them something years ago. They wanted to collect from me. Everyone else is dead or gone."

"Are you saying they're still out there looking for you even in this storm?"

"Those boys were born to do this. That's why you're my only chance."

Rick frowned and glanced behind Kemp. The men were native Alaskans, as he'd thought. The odds of survival through avoiding them had just dropped with the temperature. "I was heading to the mine shaft for protection. Do they know about that?"

"I don't know. But I guess we'll find out." Kemp's breath puffing in clouds around his head, he waved the gun at Rick. "Lead on, then."

Just keep moving. He watched the edge of the forest for any signs of the other two men who were after Kemp's gold.

"You know, you should have left the gold behind. Let them have it."

"Shut up."

"If they're that determined to catch you, they'll find us, and then what? All we can do is take cover and shoot. How much ammo do you have? I have one cartridge left in my gun and that's it."

"Shut up."

Realizing that he wouldn't be able to get Kemp to talk about the men who had attacked them, Rick decided to take a different tack. "So what did you do to get into this? The guards who worked as your miners reminded me a little of organized crime, the way they were armed to the hilt." Rick was pretty sure they were in fact part of an organized crime ring, but he wanted to hear what Kemp could tell him.

"Gambling. Throw in some loan sharks and the next thing you know, I'm offering up the gold in return for my life."

"Only there wasn't any gold."

"Huh?" Kemp trudged behind, breathing hard. "Oh, that's your brother talking. The odds were long on this claim. But that's how it is when you gamble. You never know when you're going to hit the jackpot. The possibility is always there, even if it is very remote. If only I could have had this kind of luck at the tables, then I wouldn't be here. But my grandfather wasn't any different than me. He just preferred the outdoors. He put all his money and my inheritance into mining, hoping he'd strike it rich one day. When he runs out of funds to keep the operation going, what does he do? Borrows more money against the gold that he doesn't even have yet, and then next thing I know, someone is trying to collect on *his* debt, too."

"And they're still trying to collect. If you have other claims, why not just give them that bag? Let's walk away from this free men." Rick could only hope.

Kemp didn't respond other than to gasp for breath. Rick figured the guy was struggling to walk and couldn't afford to waste energy talking about the inevitable. Alongside him, Rick trudged on, his mind drifting to Shay's sweet face when she'd told him to come back to her.

If there was a way for him to make it back to her, he didn't know what it was. One foot in front of the other, his legs growing more sluggish and numb by the minute. If he stopped now, he'd never get up.

He heard a slump behind him and whirled around, grabbing his weapon.

Kemp was facedown in the snow. Rick held his weapon at the ready and scanned the forest edge as he crept toward Kemp. Had someone taken the man down? At Kemp's prostrate form, Rick knelt down and felt his pulse. Still there, but weak. He rolled the man over and saw the blood. He'd been wounded—whether last night or during his escape, Rick didn't know, but now he was left to carry the man's dead weight. He couldn't just leave him to die from the cold or his assailants.

Life had a funny way of turning the tables. Rick dropped to his knees and rested for a minute, unsure if he had what he needed to keep going. The dreams that tormented him when he slept had nothing on this unending nightmare. He hung his head, wishing it could just be over.

Shay's face. He thought of Shay's face and her pleading eyes and got to his feet. He pulled Kemp over him in a fireman's carry, his shoulder wound burning again. He grabbed the bag of gold, noting that it weighed only a few pounds. But they were pounds that could make or break his success. The gold—the very thing they'd all fought and killed over—would have to be left behind.

He couldn't carry that and Kemp, too, with his wound, and so he dropped it. In the end, Kemp would probably kill him for it, but if it saved their lives, then that was a risk Rick was willing to take.

He paused and Kemp mumbled, then twitched. The next thing he knew, Kemp wrestled with him. Rick released the man as gently as he could to stand on his own two feet.

His eyes were wild and he punched Rick. "Where is it? Where's the gold?"

Rick shrugged, forgetting why he cared. "Sorry, man. I had to carry you or the gold. Did you want me to leave you to die?"

Kemp punched him. "I'm as good as dead without that."

He trudged back, following the footsteps that were quickly filling in with snow. Rick shrugged again and let him go, then turned his back to see to his own safety. A bullet whizzed by his ear and Rick jerked around to see Kemp waving his weapon at him. Rick could have sworn he'd removed it from the man.

"Help me or die," the wild man said.

The last of Rick's hope flickered out then. *Connor, where are you?* At least Shay had gotten to safety. He hiked toward Kemp, ready to have it out with the man and be done, but as they plodded back in the direction they'd come, there was no sign of the bag with the gold. The snow had quickly buried it just as it would them if they didn't find shelter.

Kemp turned on him, rage and madness filling his eyes. "You stole it. You hid it from me somewhere."

Rick held his numb palms out. "I don't care about the gold. What good is it if we're dead?"

Kemp aimed his gun at Rick at close range. Rick instinctively shoved the man's hand upward, and the gun went off. Rick didn't want to kill the guy if he didn't have to, but all the same, he should have known it would come to this. He pressed the muzzle of his own weapon—the gun he knew would save his life—against Kemp's shoulder and fired.

TWENTY-TWO

Shay struggled to see through the pounding snow, but she'd convinced Aiden to let her come back with him.

True to his word, he'd found another bush-country airstrip, where they'd landed and quickly got their hands on communications. Radioing for help, Aiden had called the state police and made contact with Connor, who was within minutes of landing at the gold-mining airstrip despite the inclement weather.

Connor had called for law enforcement assistance, too, but had no intention of waiting, especially with his former FBI agent brother, Reg, who now worked as security detail, along for the ride.

But she and Aiden were closer and wanted to be there. She couldn't live with herself if something happened to Rick as a result of them leaving him behind, no matter that their choices had seemed few at the time.

Aiden flew close to the ground and Shay watched the trees, searching for the airstrip. The Cessna swooped over the gorge they'd seen on the way out and that was when she saw them.

"There's Rick and…Kemp's there, too," Shay said. "It doesn't look good."

"I see them," Aiden said, frustrated worry clear in his voice. "He was supposed to find cover. Stay hidden."

"I guess it worked out pretty much as well as everything else has." She sent Aiden a glare, then watched through the window. "Hang in there, Rick. We're here. Help is coming. Oh, Lord, please help him."

"You should pray for Kemp. He's probably the one who is going to need the help."

A gunshot rang out.

"And I'm going to need help if something happens to you," Aiden added. "He's going to kill me for bringing you out here where we risk getting shot. We should go back. I was an idiot to let you come."

"You couldn't stop me."

In slow motion, Shay watched Kemp point a weapon at Rick. Rick shoved the weapon upward and they wrestled. What was the matter with them? They both acted…drugged.

"He's freezing out there, with or without bad

guys trying to kill him." Her voice trembled. "Land this thing. We have to help him."

Rick and Kemp wrestled and stumbled over the edge. Into the gorge.

Rick lay there against the snow-piled ledge, staring up at the sliver of sky at the gorge's opening. The ledge where he'd landed was a few feet down, and though it had stopped a fall to his death at the bottom of the gorge, pained emanated from his leg. He suspected it was broken. Several feet of snow had probably kept him alive, but for what—to freeze to death?

Then he remembered, somewhere in the background of his battle with Kemp, he'd heard an airplane. Was that Connor and Reg?

He turned his aching head to the side and caught sight of Kemp lying nearby—unconscious or dead, Rick didn't know.

The cold was near to taking Rick, and his consciousness edged in and out. He wasn't sure if the snow had stopped or he was dreaming, but the white stuff wasn't hitting his face anymore. Maybe he was too cold to tell.

His mind slipped into that place of terror he dreaded when he slept. The problem was he didn't think he was sleeping now—daylight was still shining down on him from above.

But overlaid across his vision of the present were visions from the past.

After the helicopter crash, he'd dragged his copilot to cover, despite his own injuries and the gunshot wound to his leg. They'd made it to the crumbled remnants of a desert brick structure. But at least they were in the shadows. The others... Where was everyone? He looked around. He couldn't be the only one. Then Rick saw what he'd not wanted to see.

His friend was almost gone. Bleeding out. Anguish strangled him. Rick maneuvered himself around and pressed his hands against the wounds to staunch the flow.

But it wasn't enough. And he was too late.

He'd been ambushed then, much like today. They'd been providing cover for ground forces and no doubt weren't the only ones who'd taken a hit. He hadn't been able to save his copilot and friend then, but Shay and Aiden had made it to safety today. He'd given himself to that task. His success in making sure it happened caused a sense of peace to settle in his soul.

The sound of a Sea Knight helicopter on a search-and-rescue mission had filled his ears that day. Was that what he heard now? He couldn't know if they would find him in the gorge, and there wasn't a way for him to let them know where to look. The Alaskan wilderness was too vast and there was too much area to cover, even when you knew the general vicinity in which to search.

That was okay. He'd done all he could do. Rick stopped struggling with the darkness that circled like a scavenger and let it take him.

Light stirred in his vision and shards of pain racked across his head. A familiar feminine voice mingled with other voices in the shadows of his mind.

Shay?

Was he dreaming? If so, this was the first good dream he'd had since… Rick's eyes fluttered open, and awareness of a deep throbbing ache coursed through his leg, through his core.

"Rick!" Shay's face filled his vision.

He was on a gurney; a Chinook rescue helicopter was mere yards away. He focused back on Shay and smiled. She cupped his face in her hands. "Rick, can you hear me?"

His smile grew, but he couldn't find the words. Had they given him something for pain?

"Rick, they have to bring your core body temperature up. Your leg is broken and I don't know what else. But you're alive." Tears dropped from her eyes onto his cheeks and burned.

They were *both* alive—himself and her. Rick had never been happier.

She pulled away.

No, come back!

"What's the matter with him? He's not saying anything," she asked someone out of his vision. Someone from the search-and-rescue team, probably.

"He's in shock. You need to move back, ma'am. Let us do our job."

"Come on, Shay." Connor's voice sounded out now.

"Rick!" she screamed as if someone was ripping her away from him. The sound tore at his heart.

Rick caught her wrist and held on. He loved her and he couldn't have asked for more than to come back to her as she'd asked, but warnings resounded in his head again.

They were right. He was in shock. He couldn't think clearly. She leaned in, responding to his touch. "I'm no good for you," he said. That was what he'd needed to say.

Then someone pulled Shay away and he was tucked into the Chinook.

Shay sat in the waiting room of Fairbanks Memorial Hospital, still wearing the oversize parka that Rick had grabbed for her during their escape from the camp. But despite the heavy insulated layers, she couldn't seem to get warm.

What was the matter with this hospital? Couldn't they turn the heat up?

She stared ahead, feeling as though she were in shock herself. She couldn't wrap her mind around the past seventy-two hours.

Voices spoke in low tones in the hallway just around the corner from where she sat.

"Is she okay?" Connor said.

"The doctor gave her a once-over and the thumbs-up. She's already given her statement to the police," Aiden answered.

She could tell they were talking about her. Apparently, they thought she couldn't hear.

"Reg's still talking to them and the FBI as well, considering the Mafia connections. The two men who initially tried to kill them were apprehended. But I'm more worried about her. She just sits there and stares. Has she been in to see Rick yet?"

"No. The only thing wrong with her is my hardheaded brother. He doesn't know a good thing when he sees one. To be fair, he's still a little out of it."

"You're probably right. I'm going to make a few calls, maybe even check in on Rick again myself, and then I'll meet you back here in half an hour, okay?"

She heard footfalls growing distant then—Connor heading away. Pressing deeper into the uncomfortable chair, she let her thoughts drift to the past.

To think, she'd become an aviation mechanic like her father, believing that tools and logic and concrete problems would let her protect herself. Because of him, she'd learned to protect her heart. In her job and in her personal life, she'd been tough and self-sufficient. A behind-the-scenes sort of person. Nobody saw her weaknesses, so no one took advantage of her.

But none of that had mattered. In the end, men had wanted her and had even tried to kill her... because she was a mechanic. In the end, Rick had broken through her fortified walls, burned right through them, cutting her open as if he was a welder and she was metal. He'd melted her heart and then with his last words to her left her softened heart to grow cold and die.

Footsteps echoed down the hallway, yanking her from her thoughts. Aiden stepped into her line of vision and handed her a steaming cup of black hospital-vending-machine coffee. She took it with a halfhearted thank-you but didn't drink. Aiden slipped into the thin-cushioned chair next to her.

"Well, the police arrested Kemp, though he's still recuperating from his injuries. Apparently, there were still a few men alive in the camp, too."

Shay nodded. That was all good, but the news didn't do a thing for her breaking heart.

I'm no good for you. Couldn't she have just died out there before having to hear that? She couldn't believe they'd gone through all of this for Rick to say those words to her, especially after he'd already told her that he loved her.

Aiden set his coffee on the side table next to him. "I can't take this anymore, Shay. Listen up. Rick has issues. You know that, right? I get that he loves you enough that he wants you to be safely away from him. But I can see that arrangement isn't going to work for either one of you. He's not doing much better than you are right now and it's not because of his leg or gunshot wound. I think you should take matters into your own hands."

Shay allowed her gaze to drift to Aiden. "What if he won't see me?"

Aiden cocked a smile. "He will. If he could see you right now, he'd know like I do that you're better off being with him. Besides, I think this whole thing has probably changed him in ways he doesn't even realize yet. I have a feeling. Ever get one of those?"

Warmth moved over her cold heart. Rick liked to use that phrase, too. He'd asked her the same thing. She had a feeling, all right, when it came to Aiden's troublesome brother. For the longest time she'd tried to ignore it, but she was done with trying to push away love.

Rick had seemed happy to see her when they'd pulled him out of that gorge and stabilized him. Almost as if his life had depended on knowing she was nearby and safe. But that was just fanciful thinking on her part. Or was it?

Shay blew out a breath. Aiden stood and held his hand out. She placed hers in it and he led her to Rick's room but kept her hidden behind him. She peeked around and saw that Rick was asleep.

Her heart stuttered at seeing him like that, all banged up, his leg raised in traction and tubes sticking out of him. He'd been through so much— Was it really the time to confront him about a future with him?

There was that voice again—familiar, feminine and loved.

Rick couldn't seem to open his eyes. He'd been dreaming about Shay and he didn't want that dream to fade. For the first time in a long time he'd had a good dream. He hadn't woken up in cold sweats or terror or in a defensive move, holding his weapon.

Maybe he'd finally overcome his nightmares. Then he remembered he was still in the hospital bed, and the drugs had probably kept his nightmares at bay.

I wonder...

He turned his head to the sound of her voice and languished in the dream. He thought he was addicted to that voice. To her. Rick forced his eyes open and looked into her mountain-blue irises, that perfect face framed by short, spunky auburn hair, and suddenly he couldn't breathe.

Somewhere behind him, his heart rate spiked on the monitor. Shay's eyes widened. "Rick? Are you okay? I need to get help. Nurse!" she called. She slid from the chair to stand, to leave, but Rick reached out and caught her hand.

"I'm okay." He smiled.

Shay slowly sat back down, scooting the chair closer. She ran her hand down his cheek. "Please, don't shut me out. Don't tell me that you're not good for me."

His throat constricted. He knew what she was saying to him without so many words. She wanted a future with him. Same as he did with her. But he was still afraid of hurting her. Maybe he'd gotten past the worst of the night terrors, but that didn't mean all his problems were over. "Are you sure?"

She smiled, her eyes glistening with unshed tears. "I'm sure."

He'd let the nightmare go. Maybe he could let

some of his doubts go, as well. "Good. Because I don't think I can live without you by my side."

It took a few seconds for her mind to wrap around that one—he could tell. Understanding finally swelled in her eyes, permeated her face. "Is that a proposal, Mr. Savage?"

The heart-rate monitor went crazy again. "It is. I want you as my wife, to have, hold and… protect." He tugged her close, surprised he had enough strength in him, and ran his fingers through the red hair that drove him crazy. Bringing her face near, inching her lips closer, he kissed Shay long and hard. The depth of the love he felt for this woman astounded him. He would no longer keep it hidden inside because he was afraid.

"Are you sure this isn't just the painkillers talking?" she asked.

"I've known you for two years," he said. "Tried to stop thinking about you for two years. From the first moment I saw you, I had a feeling…."

* * * * *

Dear Reader,

Shay and Rick are sent on a journey that turns into much more than either of them expected. Sound familiar? The extreme circumstances force each of them to face issues from their past. The protective barriers they've built over a lifetime to guard themselves are knocked over and out of the way. Often it's through trials that we learn to overcome. Through trials that our faith in God grows, as well as our faith in each other. Such is the case for Rick and Shay in *Wilderness Peril*.

Romans 5:3–5 says: "And not only this, but we also exult in our tribulations, knowing that tribulation brings about perseverance; and perseverance, proven character; and proven character, hope; and hope does not disappoint, because the love of God has been poured out within our hearts through the Holy Spirit who was given to us."

While I was writing the last couple of chapters and then finally typed the last line, the song "Overcome," as sung by Jeremy Camp, was drifting through my thoughts and heart, and I could almost believe that Rick was singing along. I pray the Lord speaks to your heart through this story, and for His blessings in your life.

I love to hear from my readers. Please visit my website, www.elizabethgoddard.com, to learn about how you can connect with me.

Blessings!
Elizabeth Goddard

Questions For Discussion

1. Shay was an aircraft mechanic, which is a male-dominated field. Have you experienced, or do you know someone who has experienced, working in a career dominated by the opposite gender? Discuss.

2. Could you relate to Shay's need to fit in with her fellow male employees? Why or why not?

3. Rick held a traumatic experience from his past deep inside, so much so that it always seeped out the cracks at the wrong time and place. Has there ever been a struggle in your life that you tried to work through by yourself? How did you deal with it?

4. Shay and Rick have worked together for two years and knew each other to a certain point. Add to that, Shay knew he held something inside, and she was afraid to trust him completely. Have you ever known someone with a secret that made you uncomfortable? How did you handle things?

5. Shay was pushed past her comfort zone when she traveled to the Alaskan bush. What

activities would move you out of your comfort zone? Discuss.

6. Although Rick's brother didn't show up for their meeting, he believed in his brother and knew that he must be in trouble, despite the fact that Aiden had a past as an unreliable person. Do you know someone you struggle to count on? Why or why not?

7. In the story, Rick thought about the fact that during his experiences as a marine, he turned to God, but his brother, Aiden, eventually turned to alcohol. Discuss why you think some people turn to God when they go through struggles and others to substance abuse.

8. When Rick's brother, Aiden, didn't show up at their meeting place, Rick didn't immediately think the worst of him. He didn't stop believing that his brother would find a way to overcome his troubles and find his way to God. Can you relate to Rick in this? Why or why not?

9. Buster Kemp was a man who dug himself deep and had to pay off a debt to dangerous people or die. He was following in his grandfather's footsteps, carrying on the fam-

ily legacy, if you will, of gambling away a fortune he didn't have. Unfortunately, he dragged more people into his death trap. Have you ever known anyone like Buster in this regard? Discuss how bad habits, whether they run in the family or not, can devastate lives.

10. Rick saw Shay as the company aircraft mechanic, as a tough, hard-as-nails woman because that was what Shay held up for everyone to see. Do you think Rick would have respected her less if she'd been more willing to reveal her softer feminine side at the Deep Horizon hangar? Why or why not?

11. Discuss how you view men and women, and society's norms when it comes to gender-based roles in employment.

12. At the mining camp, Rick and Shay were coerced into cooperating. They didn't really have a lot of choice, though action movies would have us believe Rick could have simply snatched up a weapon and shot his way out of the camp. How well do you think Rick and Shay handled things? What would you have done differently?

3. Has there ever been a time when you were in an unbearable, no-win situation? What did you do?

4. How did you feel when Rick shot the man who was about to shoot Shay? Do you think he did the right thing?

5. In the end, Rick stayed behind so that his brother and the woman he loved could escape. Rick was ready and willing to give his life for others. He was a hero. Have you ever known a real hero? Talk about the heroes in your life.

LARGER-PRINT BOOKS!

GET 2 FREE
LARGER-PRINT NOVELS
PLUS 2 FREE
MYSTERY GIFTS

Love Inspired.
SUSPENSE
RIVETING INSPIRATIONAL ROMAN⬛

Larger-print novels are now available...